"YOU WANT TO TALK OR SCREW FIRST?"

"You don't waste words, do you, Fargo?" she said.

"Nope."

"What if I said you're being rude and inexcusably presumptuous?" she frowned.

"Say it," Fargo shot back.

Her eyes stayed on him, narrowed a fraction. "I don't like crudeness," she said.

"I don't like games." He drained the bourbon, kept his eyes hard upon her.

She leaned forward, her deep, full breasts rising to the very edge of the neckline. "I think we've talked enough for now," she murmured.

"Just what I was thinking," Fargo said, his hands reaching out for her . . .

Exciting Adult Westerns by Jon Sharpe from SIGNET

THE TRAILSMAN '3

MOUNTAIN MAN KILL

by

Jon Sharpe

A SIGNET BOOK
NEW AMERICAN LIBRARY
TIMES MIRROR

NAL BOOKS ARE AVAILABLE AT QUANTITY DISCOUNTS
WHEN USED TO PROMOTE PRODUCTS OR SERVICES. FOR
INFORMATION PLEASE WRITE TO PREMIUM MARKETING DIVISION,
THE NEW AMERICAN LIBRARY, INC., 1633 BROADWAY,
NEW YORK, NEW YORK 10019.

The first chapter of this book appeared in *The Hanging Trail*,
the second volume of this series.

SIGNET TRADEMARK REG. U.S. PAT. OFF. AND FOREIGN COUNTRIES
REGISTERED TRADEMARK—MARCA REGISTRADA
HECHO EN CHICAGO, U.S.A.

SIGNET, SIGNET CLASSICS, MENTOR, PLUME, MERIDIAN AND NAL
BOOKS are published by The New American Library, Inc.,
1633 Broadway, New York, New York 10019

First Printing, August, 1980

6   7   8   9   10   11   12

PRINTED IN THE UNITED STATES OF AMERICA

The Trailsman

Beginnings . . . they bend the tree and they mark the man. Skye Fargo was born when he was eighteen. Terror was his midwife, vengeance his first cry. Killing spawned Skye Fargo, ruthless, cold-blooded murder. Out of the acrid smoke of gunpowder still hanging in the air, he rose, cried out a promise never forgotten.

The Trailsman, they began to call him all across the West, searcher, scout, hunter, the man who could see where others only looked, his skills for hire but not his soul, the man who lived each day to the fullest, yet trailed each tomorrow. Skye Fargo, the Trailsman, the seeker who could take the wildness of a land and the wanting of a woman and make them his own.

Summer, 1861,
the north Wyoming Territory
at the foot of the Grand Tetons
and the Wind River Mountains.

1

"Going to stay here a spell?" the girl asked, hope in her voice. The big black-haired man with the lake-blue eyes shook his head slowly and saw the moment of disappointment touch the girl's face.

"Sorry," he remarked, and she gave a little half-shrug in return. She sat across the table from him in the town's only saloon and hotel, but she wasn't a saloon girl and he liked that. She was fresher, softer, more natural. And hungrier. That much had been in her eyes the very first moment they exchanged glances. That was only yesterday, he reminded himself, after he'd arrived in Wind River with the supply train he'd brought all the way up from Kansas. She was working in the general store when he had stopped there for saddle soap and there'd been no false coyness about her, and he liked that, too. She'd agreed to a drink with him last night without hesitation and now she was across from him again in the noisy saloon-lobby.

"Wind River isn't much of a town for staying in," he said quietly, and she allowed a small, rueful smile.

"I guess not. It needs a lot of growing yet," she said.

Skye Fargo glanced out the window behind where they were sitting. Her answer had been an understatement. The Wind River Mountains rose up just beyond the edge of the town, rugged, towering, glaring down. Two things came out of those vast mountains and onto the town. In winter, the roaring blizzards, and in the spring and fall, the roaring mountain men. Wind River was a fur-trading town, a place where the mountain men came to sell their precious pelts to the agents for the fur companies. The Rocky Mountain Fur Company had an agent in Wind River. Hudson Bay was thinking of one, he'd heard, but that company was plenty busy with the Northwest-Canadian territory. A handful of ranches bordered the town on the southern end, and a trail of silver miners used it as a stopping place. That was Wind River, a trading post masquerading as a town.

He brought his eyes back to the girl in front of him. Jenny Lindhof, a slender figure in red and white calico, small-waisted, with breasts that seemed high and pointy under the folds of her dress. She had a face, small-featured, that bordered on being waiflike, yet was somehow very appealing, with hazel eyes that were level and forthright. Not really his kind of woman, ordinarily, yet something had sparked between them the moment they'd met. Besides, it had been a long, hard trip, too long without a woman.

"How'd you come to Wind River, Jenny?" he asked.

"I was in Dry Creek—that's some sixty miles south—When my pa died," she answered. "He was a silver grubber. I'd no place to go and no money. When Mr. Axelson asked me to come here and work in his store, I just up and came."

His eyes studied her for a moment. "You're a funny little creature, Jenny Lindhof," Skye Fargo said, not ungently. "You'd fit in at any church social, but you've come here with me easy as any dance-hall girl."

She gazed back at him as she thought about his words. "I guess it seems that way," she said. "My pa taught me to take things when they come your way.

2

You're an uncommonly good-looking man, Skye Fargo. Most of those who come to Wind River are more animal than human. A girl gets tired waiting. Tired and feeling wasted."

Her small, thin-fingered hand disappeared under his as he patted it. "Your kind of honesty needs matching, Jenny," he said. "I'm not thinking about holding hands or long-time courtin'."

Her smile held something he'd never seen before: shyness and satisfaction at the same time. "I didn't figure you were," she said softly.

He leaned back, returned the smile. She was indeed a surprising little thing, this new friend, yet instantly likable, he decided, and that was rare enough, too. He turned, called the waitress over, and told her to leave the bottle. He glanced at four men coming into the big room through the front swinging doors and then returned his attention to Jenny Lindhof. He was pouring another drink for both of them when he became aware of the figures moving toward the table; he glanced up, saw the men bearing down on him. He put the bottle down and watched them approach. The first one was tall, swaggering, wearing hardness with the pride of the cruel. The three close behind him were sweat-stained cowhands, one with dull eyes, one with a flattened nose, and the last one slack-jawed, his eyes intent on Jenny Lindhof.

The hard-faced one halted as Skye sat back. "You Skye Fargo?" the man asked harshly.

"I might be," Fargo returned.

"I'm Brody, foreman for the Harry Stanton Agency. The boss wants to see you," the man said.

Fargo frowned, cast a glance at Jenny. "Who's Harry Stanton?" he asked, saw Jenny start to answer, but the man's voice cut her off.

"Agent for the Rocky Mountain Fur Company," Brody snapped.

Fargo nodded, the name clicking in his mind. "Yes, I passed the place coming into town," he said.

3

"The boss said to bring you back with us," the man continued.

Fargo allowed him a tight smile. "Sorry. I've other plans for tonight. Try me in a day or so, if I'm still here," he said, and turned from the men.

He felt a hand come down upon his shoulder. "Tonight," the man said. "The boss sent us to find you and bring you back."

Fargo glanced at the man's hand, brought his eyes up to the man's hard face. He let Brody watch his eyes turn from soft lake-blue to blue quartz. "You've got a half-second to get your hand off there, cousin," Fargo said in almost a whisper.

The man hesitated, then let his hand drop away. "The boss don't take to being turned down," the foreman said.

"Then it'll be somethin' new for him," Fargo replied. He let his eyes flick over the other three men and then back to the foreman, saw the man watch his hand come to rest on the butt of the big Colt .45 in his holster. "Good evening, gents," Fargo said with cold affability. He saw the foreman, Brody, hesitate again, his hard face twitching, then watched the man turn, gesture to the other three to fall back. The quartet shuffled off and Fargo turned back to the girl. He heard the breath escape from between her lips.

"Exactly who is this Stanton?" he asked her.

"Mister Big in the fur-trading business. Most of the mountain men sell to his outfit," Jenny told him.

"How the hell did he know I was in town?" Fargo frowned.

"I guess you've got a name," she said.

The big, black-haired man gave a grunt. Her words were too true. He was always surprised at how many knew the name of Skye Fargo, the Trailsman. Too many, sometimes, such as just now. Too many who wanted his special talents, too many who'd heard too much, some of it pulled out of shape, some of it true.

"Let's go to my room, Jenny," Skye said, closing one

4

big hand around the neck of the bottle. "We won't be bothered there."

The shy little smile came at once, but she rose to follow him as he threaded his way through the tables of the hotel saloon-lobby. Foreman Brody and his crew had decided to drown their failure in a corner of the room, he saw, and he caught Brody's quick glance as he led Jenny up the stairs. His room was at the far end of a dim hallway, close to the top of the back stairway. He opened the door, turned the lamp on low, and Jenny stepped inside. He saw her glance take in the only furniture in the room: a single chair, a battered dresser, and the brass bed. She turned, and he helped her take off the small shawl she wore about her shoulders.

Jenny Lindhof seemed suddenly so small, all the waiflike quality returning to her, and he found himself hesitant, her eyes giving him no sign. He saw no expectation, desire, no invitation, yet there was no reproof, either, just a wide and waiting expression. He was still trying to read her when she lifted herself up on tiptoe and kissed him gently on the mouth.

"Thanks," she said, and he waited. "For not wanting to treat me like a dance-hall girl."

He smiled. "You're very different, Jenny," he said, leaned down, and pressed his mouth to hers. Her lips, thin, suddenly seemed to expand and her mouth opened, little pulling movements drawing him in deeper. He felt the fire flame at once in his loins. Slowly, he pushed her back onto the bed, set the bottle on the floor beside one of the brass legs. Her lips reached up for his again as he sat down beside her. Gently, he let his hand push the calico dress from her shoulder. Her hand came up and he watched her fingers pull open buttons. The dress came free, slipped from her shoulders altogether, and he pulled it down to her waist. The high, round breasts were no larger than he'd suspected, but still deliciously inviting, full and firm and fresh as new-bloomed partridge berries. Her arms came around his neck and he took one full little breast in his mouth as she pushed his shirt open and off. He unbuckled his gun belt, let it fall to the floor where he heard it slide under the bed.

He pulled gently on the breast and felt her back arch. "Oh, my, oh, oh, oh, my," she whispered in rhythm with his caressing lips. She pushed up to help his mouth take in more of her and he felt the rest of the calico dress slip off, paused, drew back for a moment. Her body was without an ounce of extra flesh, a young girl's body, flat stomach and long rib cage, but the dark triangle startlingly large and thick. She pulled his chest down atop her, his mouth back upon her breasts as she cried out again, small words of instant ecstasy. Her hands were moving down his back, nails tracing a sharp line that excited with its hint of pain. He didn't hear the click of the door opening as she ran little sounds together, but the harsh voice shattered the fevered beginnings with malicious delight.

"Now, ain't it a shame to break in on this," Fargo heard the voice say, recognized the foreman's rasp at once. He heard Jenny's gasp, felt her arms tighten around him, her body grow taut as a coiled spring.

"Easy. Relax," he whispered to her, and in a moment felt her drop back onto the bed. He half-turned, his body still mostly over hers. Brody was standing with a revolver in hand, grinning, the other three behind him.

"That's right, Fargo, just back off the little lady," the foreman drawled.

"Yeah, let's have a good look at her." The flat-nosed one laughed.

Fargo didn't move, except to let his ice-blue eyes flick coldly over the three men.

"You ain't hardly started yet, anyway," Brody jeered. "You're out but not in." He laughed coarsely at his own words.

Fargo turned a fraction more, still covering most of the girl with his body. His eyes, blue slits, measured

6

the distance to the gun held casually in Brody's hand. The other three had their guns still holstered.

"Get up, Fargo. You're goin' with us," Brody snapped, his voice growing hard.

"I'll stay here and finish for you," the slack-jawed one added eagerly. Fargo moved a fraction more. His right hand, half under his body, gathered the top bedsheet into a ball inside his fist.

"I guess you boys win," he remarked, and the men saw the powerful torso begin to slowly push up from Jenny Lindhof's nude body. Brody sneered as he grunted. He was still encased in his own smugness when Fargo's hard-muscled figure catapulted sideways and, with the same motion, snapped the bedsheet like a whip. The sheet wrapped itself around Brody's forearm and gun, and Fargo yanked hard at the same instant. The foreman jerked forward off balance and Fargo's left came around in an arc to catch him on the side of the jaw. The blow sent him crashing head-first into the brass of the foot of the bed. He hadn't slid down to the floor yet as Fargo dived over him, crashing into the nearest two intruders. He brought both down with him in a tangle of bodies as the fourth one drew his gun in panic. Fargo rolled, seizing the slack-jawed one with him, as the shot slammed into the wood of the floorboards.

"Goddamn," he heard the man curse. Fargo, on his back, held the slack-jawed one over him with one hand around the man's neck. He twisted with his human shield as the gunman tried to find a clear shot; then, bringing up his other hand, Fargo pushed with all his strength. The slack-jawed man's body rose, arched backward, and fell into the other two, who twisted away in an automatic reaction. Another shot rang out, this one plowing harmlessly into the ceiling. But the Trailsman had bought the split second he wanted, enough time to reach the whiskey bottle and fling it. It smashed into the flat-nosed face of the one brandishing his gun; the man staggered backward,

7

shouting in pain, dropping his gun to wipe at the cascade of blood that erupted from his face.

Fargo dived again, low, slamming into the nearest pair of legs, and the man went down. Fargo swung at once, felt his hand connect with flesh and bone, heard the oath of pain. The man landed half atop him, and Fargo used his shoulders to drive him backward. He sank his fist deep into a belly made fat by too much beer and heard the man gasp out breath as he drew his legs up in pain, half-turning on his side. Fargo yanked the gun from his holster just as the foreman, Brody, pulled his bloodied head up. Fargo saw the man's hand come up with the gun in it, and the black-haired man fired instantly. The shot caught the foreman at the bottom of his neck and his head fell forward, driving the spurting red down onto his chest.

Fargo whirled, the bellow of pain and rage exploding to his right, looked up in time to see the flat-nosed man roaring at him, face streaked with blood, but the jagged neck of the bottle clutched in one hand. As the wild, red-stained figure leaped at him, the piece of bottle held outstretched in one hand, Fargo flattened himself to the floor, rolled, felt the man's figure catapult over him. He kicked out as the man's legs followed, flipped the figure upward. He heard the harshly guttural cry that ended in a gagging sound as the man came down on the jagged piece of glass in his own hand.

Fargo spun again, saw the slack-jawed one on all fours, shaking his head to clear it. The fourth man half-stumbled, half-fell as he tried to reach the door. Fargo leaped up, caught him as his hand closed around the doorknob. He slammed into the man with all his strength and heard the sharp crack of a wrist bone and the scream of pain that followed. The figure slumped to the floor, crying in agony, curling his legs up under him. Fargo turned from him, grabbed the last of the quartet, spun his slack-jawed face around. Stark fear was in the man's eyes.

8

"Jesus, no, don't kill me," the man sputtered.

Fargo kept his grip on the man. "I'd as soon put a hole through you as the other two," he rasped. "But I want you able to go back and tell your boss what his stupid gunslingers tried to do." He flung the man away, turned to the one holding his limp wrist in pain, rocking back and forth on his knees. He yanked the man forward, ignoring his cry of pain and fear mixed together, flung him half atop the slack-jawed one. "Both of you, take those other two with you. You'll find somebody to bury them. You tell your boss how it was, you hear me, bastard?" he barked, kicked the man in the leg. The man nodded vigorously as he pulled himself to his feet.

The sound of voices and footsteps gathered outside the door. Fargo found Jenny with a quick glance, huddled in one corner, her calico dress held in front of her, then opened the door. The hotel clerk, the bartender, and a half-dozen others had come upstairs.

"It's all over," Fargo said, stepped back as the two men dragged the body of the foreman out of the room, then did the same with the other red-stained, slashed body. "Some folks got the wrong ideas into their heads," Fargo said quietly. He saw the bartender and a few of the other men move to help carry the two dead bodies down the back stairs. The hotel clerk started to turn away when Fargo reached out to him.

"I'll need another room," Fargo said matter-of-factly. "This one's going to need a good cleaning in the morning."

The clerk stared at him for a moment. Wind River was a town used to violence, but this big black-haired man meted it out with icy efficiency. "Room Ten, just down the hall," the clerk said. "It's yours, sir."

"Thanks," Fargo said calmly, watched the man hurry away, and closed the door, turned to Jenny, who still clutched the dress to her. "Slip it on. We're going down the hall to another room," he said. Her eyes, wide, unmoving, stayed on him, but he saw her

9

shudder; he reached out to her, drew her against him, held her until she stopped trembling. He looked down at the round, hazel eyes. " 'Less you'd rather I took you back home," he offered, waited, retrieved his own gun and holster.

"I'd just sit there and still be scared," she said. She stepped back, slipped the dress on in one quick motion, and followed him as he led the way down the hall to the other room. He closed the door behind them, bolted it this time.

"We won't be bothered again," he told her. She sank down onto the brass bed, almost a twin of the other one except for its own set of scratches. He sat down beside her and pressed her back onto the bed, kissed her gently. She made no response for a few moments, and then he felt her lips opening, growing softer, returning the pressure. He helped her wriggle out of the dress and undid his own clothes. His eyes took in the narrow-hipped figure again. Jenny Lindhof, naked, seemed more waif than woman, except for the thick, luxuriant triangle. He bent down, gently taking one round, high, little-girl breast in his mouth.

Her gasp was instant, and he felt her hands press upon the back of his neck. He let his tongue move slowly in circles around the tiny tip, felt it harden instantly, and once again she pushed upward to give him all of the breast. Her hands moved from his neck, down along his body, tracing a feverish path down to the risen shaft that awaited her. As her hands closed around it, he heard her little cry of delight and she half-turned, drew her breast from his lips. She swung herself in a half-circle, head bent down to the male hardness of him, using both hands to caress and stroke. He heard the little sounds, almost a whimpered laugh, that came from her as she put her face against him, rubbed her cheeks over his eternal symbol. Then he felt the warm moistness enclose him as her lips caressed. Tiny sounds of delight came from her, pure and filled with pleasure and discovery. Fi-

10

nally she drew back, a shudder going through her body, and then he felt her legs moving over onto him. She lowered herself over him, slowly, crying out in ecstasy as she moved her torso up and down in her own rhythm. She leaned forward for him to pull upon the high little mounds and her hands played up and down his sides. He let her indulge in everything she wanted, and he then rolled her to the side, then onto her back, and her legs clasped around him at once, drawing him into her with fervent anxiety.

"Oh, Fargo, oh, oh," she cried out with his every movement, words joining rhythm to form a song of ecstasy until suddenly she screamed and clasped herself to him, to cling there until the shattering moment subsided. She lay back on the bed, her eyes fastened on him, the shy little smile suddenly touching her lips, the hint of satisfaction in it once again.

"You're a surprising little thing, Jenny," he said, pressing his face against the high little-girl breasts.

"Make the most of your moments, Pa always said. You never know how long it'll be between," she answered. She lay beside him for but a short while and then she began to once more make the most of her moment, exploring pleasures in her own ways, a small, thin monument of high-wire sexuality. Finally she slept with arms tight around him until the morning sun rose high enough to slide into the room. He opened his eyes to see her devouring his body with her eyes. "Just want to make sure I remember everything," she said to him. Her fingers touched the half-moon scar on his forearm and her glance questioned.

"Bear claw. Grizzly," he told her, and she gave a tiny shudder. She rose, up into a sitting position, brushing her breasts across his lips as she did.

"I open the store this morning," she said, swinging from the bed.

He watched her as she hurried across to the little bathroom, small, flat rear, all slenderness and almost boyish from the back. He heard her wash and then

11

she came out, glistening, the lithe young-girl look of her terribly appealing. She slipped on clothes, stood dressed in moments, a smallish, very proper and demure-looking young girl, and he found himself thinking of Jenny Lindhof in the night. The outside of a package could certainly mislead one, he reflected wryly.

"When will you leave town?" she asked with her open, level eyes.

He shrugged. "Have to pick up the rest of my pay for the wagon trip this afternoon," he said.

"Then you're on your way?" she asked.

"Pretty much," he said, got to his feet, and went to her, cupping her face with one big hand. "If I stay, you'll be the first to know." She smiled. "You're an unusual little package, Jenny. Someone worth your while will pass through here someday."

"Maybe. Someday," she said. "Meanwhile, I'll have this to remember. I'll make it last. It was all it ought to be." She reached up, kissed him quickly, turned to the door. "Don't come to me 'less you plan to stay awhile," she said, pausing, her small face grave. "That'd be too much to handle."

"I understand," he said, and knew he'd abide by her request. She was too nice a person to use. She disappeared out the door and he dressed slowly, putting his gun belt on last. He emerged into the hallway, paused, his eyes searching the area. He didn't figure the two from last night to come back. They'd had more than enough. But they could have equally stupid friends. He moved down the hallway, hand on the butt of the Colt .45, relaxed as he went downstairs and paid the clerk for the room. The bar-lobby was empty save for an elderly black man sweeping the floor and one waitress cleaning tables. The sun, strong, now, came in through the windows. Fargo stepped outside, his eyes squinting down the main street of Wind River. A half-dozen platform drays lined up taking on supplies. Silver grubbers. They'd move on along the lower reaches of the Grand Tetons, searching, forever searching. Damn few of them finding.

Beyond the end of town, the Wind River Mountains rose up, an awesome green wall, vibrant and throbbing. The mountain men weren't the only ones who trapped and hunted the vast area. The Indians also hunted the Wind River Mountains, made summer camps in the fertile bountifulness, mostly Arapaho and Cheyenne, with some Poncas and Northern Shoshoni. He took his eyes from the mountains, started off the front step of the hotel to make his way down to the Two Fork Supply Company for the balance of his pay for delivering the supply train from Kansas. He'd only taken a half-dozen long, loping steps when a woman's voice called out from behind him, a touch of arrogance in her tone.

"Mister Fargo! Just a minute, please!" the voice said.

The big man turned, pushed a lock of black hair from his forehead and focused his gaze on the woman as she stepped from the edge of the hotel building. His eyes took in a tall woman clothed in a maroon silk jacket over a matching skirt. A full, deep bosom pushed out a white silk blouse from under her jacket. His eyes paused at her face, even features, gray-blue eyes, and a pair of thin high eyebrows that gave her an air of constant haughtiness. A good-looking woman, he decided, with her brown hair pulled back in a bun, good-looking and very self-assured, her gray-blue eyes doing their own piece of instant assessment. "I'd like to talk to you," she added.

"Seems I'm awful popular around here," Fargo remarked.

"I owe you an apology," the woman said. "I'm Caroline Stanton. I sent my foreman and his men to find you last night. I told Brody to ask you to come see me, that's all. The rest was his doing. He's always been a stupid man, forever needing to prove something. Frankly, I won't miss him."

"Me neither," Fargo agreed flatly.

13

Caroline Stanton offered a smile, coolly warm. "I apologize again for his actions," she said. "But I do want to talk to you. But not here. Will you come out to my ranch?"

Fargo eyed Caroline Stanton. In her early thirties, he guessed, the self-assured poise of a woman used to being obeyed. "I thought Harry Stanton was agent for the Rocky Mountain Fur Company," he said.

"My husband hasn't been a well man for over a year. I run the agency now. He only makes occasional trips down to Casper. He's on one now, in fact." Her eyes traveled up and down the big man's long hard frame. "Will you come?" she asked again. "I promise it won't be a waste of your time." The gray-blue eyes held his, eyes saying so much more than her lips. "Shall we say this evening?" she pressed.

He shrugged agreement. He seldom denied his natural curiosity, especially where good-looking women were concerned. For a grubby little trading-post town, Wind River was turning into an interesting place. Caroline Stanton read the shrug correctly and smiled. "Head west from town, take the road to the right out by the big oak," she said. "I'll expect you at eight."

He caught the subtle change in her tone on the last sentence. She was used to giving orders. "Expect me when I get there," he said casually.

Caroline Stanton's eyebrows arched as she nodded understanding of the unsaid. "Of course," she replied quietly, allowing him a small smile. He watched her walk to a buckboard, climb in, and drive off without a glance backward. She drove the buckboard with easy assurance, sitting straight on the seat. He imagined she did everything with that certain authority, everything done her way. Maybe it was time she learned a different tune. He turned, sauntered down to the Two Fork Supply Company, where the balance of his pay awaited him. The paymaster didn't show until most of the morning was gone, but finally the business was done and Fargo put most of the money

14

into a heavy envelope and went to the hotel, which also served as the post drop. One thing Wind River did have was a regular post service as a trading-post town. He addressed an envelope and paid the post fee, left it with the hotel clerk for the next mail rider.

He next strolled to the town stable, took out his pinto, led the horse to a water tank, conscious of the curious glances drawn by the pinto. An Ovaro, with the striking pattern of solid black head, neck, fore-quarters, and hindquarters, and gleaming white in between, the horse always commanded attention, even from those who didn't especially take to pintos. Fargo spent the rest of the day giving the pinto a good scrubbing and currying the horse thoroughly. He sure needed it. The trip had been a hot and dusty trek, and besides, Fargo liked riding a clean, fresh horse.

It was nearly dark when he finished, and he rode back past the warehouse of the Rocky Mountain Fur Company. Two worn old-timers slowly sorted a few pelts and Fargo glimpsed the emptiness of the warehouse building through the wide-open doors. By the summer's end, the warehouse would be bulging with furs as, one by one, the mountain men and Indian trappers would come in bringing their season's catch. Fargo rode on back to the hotel, steering clear of the general store and Jenny Lindhof. He then had something to eat and sat in on a poker game to kill further time. Finally, he rode out of town and headed west under a canopy of bright summer stars. He found the big oak, turned right, and kept moving forward. It was about eight-thirty when the low outline of the Stanton ranch appeared, windows lighted in the main house and the bunkhouse behind it. The door to the house opened as he was tying the pinto to the hitching rail.

Caroline Stanton stood framed in the doorway in a floor-length gown. The yellow light behind her outlined the long curve of her legs and thighs through the filmy material. She stepped back as he went inside, pushed the door closed behind him. The dress,

15

he saw, was salmon-colored silk, smooth and thin so that it clung to her as she moved. A square-cut low neckline let her deep breasts rise up invitingly. She had perhaps ten to fifteen pounds extra weight, he decided, but it was evenly distributed and only added to the well-fleshed, womanly handsomeness of her. The quiet, half-amused assurance was again noticeable in her blue-gray eyes.

"Drink?" she asked, stopping at a silver serving cart on wheels. "You look like a bourbon man."

"Bourbon's fine, with a little ice and water," Fargo said. He glanced around the room as she poured the drink. No poor man's house, yet nothing overly showy either, good, solid furniture and heavy velvet drapes in dark red. She gestured to a leather sofa, sat down beside him, half-turning to face him. Her left breast pushed up dangerously and deliciously at the edge of the low-cut neckline.

"I'm glad you kept your word to come," Caroline Stanton said.

"I always keep my word," Fargo remarked.

"So I've heard," the woman said.

Fargo sipped on his bourbon. "How'd you know I was in town, Mrs. Stanton?" he asked.

"Please call me Caroline," the woman said. "Charley Myers told me he'd hired you to bring his supply wagons in from Kansas."

"That's right. He wanted me to find a new route. The Cheyenne have been waiting for him the last few times," Fargo said.

"He told me he'd met you in Kansas and offered you the deal," Caroline Stanton said.

"It was a job." Fargo shrugged, sipped the bourbon.

"I'd heard you didn't take jobs just for the money," Caroline said, lifting her fine-lined eyebrows.

"Not usually," he agreed. "You heard right. But an old friend's widow was needing hard cash. I took the job for some extra to send her."

16

"My, a heart of gold, besides," she said, and he caught the faint mocking in her voice.

"No, just old friends and old favors," Fargo returned, pulled hard on his drink, and turned eyes edged with ice on her. "You want to talk more or screw first," he said.

The mocking left her voice at once. "You don't waste words, do you?" Caroline Stanton said.

"Nope."

"What if I said you're being rude and inexcusably presumptuous?" She frowned.

"Say it," Fargo shot back.

Her eyes stayed on him, narrowed a fraction. "I don't like crudeness," she said.

"I don't like games." He drained the bourbon, kept his eyes hard on her.

He saw her lips tighten for an instant, then the wry smile follow as she sat back. "Talk, first," she said, drawing on her drink.

"Start," he snapped.

"The agency is having trouble, bad trouble," Caroline Stanton said almost angrily. "Our lifeblood as a business is being drained." He sat back, his eyes waiting. "Most all the mountain men sell their furs here to us. We have agreements with most of them to bring their pelts to us."

"Agreements?" Fargo cut in.

"Verbal understandings, of course. Most of the mountain men can't read or write, as you know. But as agent for the Rocky Mountain Fur Company we offer the best prices for their furs," Caroline said.

Fargo grunted inside himself. The best was damned little compared to what the company got for the pelts. "So you've most of the mountain men in your pocket. What's the problem?" he asked.

"We're being cut out. Somebody's getting our furs," the woman snapped. "When the mountain men start to come down out of the mountains, they're intercepted, met by somebody who pays them for their furs and takes their whole catch. They come into

17

town to live it up on what they've been paid and show us a receipt they were told is from the agency."

"Which is a phony, of course," Fargo said.

"A complete phony. Some didn't even have our name on them. But the mountain men can't read. They have their cash and a receipt, and that's enough for them. They're damn touchy to work with. You can't tell them they're stupid and they've been tricked or you'll lose your head for it. But, as I said, the life-blood of the business is being drained, and it's been getting worse. Another season and we'll be out of business."

"Why don't you go out to meet the mountain men when it's time?" Fargo asked.

"We tried that. But we haven't enough men, and all it did was cut down a little on the loss. We still lost more than half our season's furs." Caroline Stanton reached over, poured herself another drink, and he offered his glass to be refreshed. "If those damn mountain men could read, they wouldn't be taken in like children, but they're so stupid," she snapped.

"Stupid enough to make you rich with their furs," Fargo returned.

Caroline Stanton glared at him for a moment, then let her eyes soften. "Your round, Fargo," she said quietly.

"You've got a problem, all right," Fargo said, turning the glass in his hand. "Got any ideas who's giving it to you?"

"Craig Bowers," she said instantly. "He operates a small outfit that's grown awfully prosperous the last few seasons. We've kept watch on him, but we haven't been able to prove anything. Furs are furs, and who can recognize them after a spell?"

"You expect I can see more than you can?" Fargo questioned.

"No, but you can do something else. There's only one way to stop this, and that's to catch them at it. They've got to be caught in the act. I need a mountain man who can do that," Caroline Stanton said.

"You must be loco." Fargo frowned.

"No. I need a mountain man who can read and write, a mountain man who'll know what's going on and nail them at it. I need someone who can play the role all the way, someone who can hunt and trap and fool them completely until they make their move. I need you."

Fargo met her gaze. "I'm not much for hunting and trapping unless it's for food," he said.

"But you can, and you're not known around here. You can be the mountain man I need. You can play the role, carry it off until they come to you and tip their hand," the woman said. "I'm offering one thousand dollars in gold coins, Fargo."

Skye heard the low whistle that escaped his lips. "That's not the kind of money a man turns down easy," he admitted.

"I hope it isn't," she said. She leaned forward, her deep full breasts rising to the very edge of the neckline. "I think we've talked enough for now," she murmured.

"Just what I was thinking," Fargo said, his hand reaching out, passing over the curving mound. Her skin was soft and creamy. He moved his hand again, but she pulled back.

"Not here," she said, rising, holding one hand out to him. He took it and followed into a sitting room, crossed it with her to a wide-windowed bedroom with a large bed in the center. Moonlight streamed in the big window to give the room a pale silver-blue tint. Caroline Stanton wriggled her shoulders free of her gown as he dropped his gun belt. He watched the silk dress cascade down past her hips, slide over her thighs, and fall at her feet. She wore nothing at all beneath it, and she stood before him, beckoning with the full-figured beauty that was hers, womanly, fashioned in ample strokes. He came to her and she clasped arms around him, pulled him with her onto the bed. She let him kiss the deep, heavy breasts and

19

she cried out, half-turned, caught his hand as he moved it down over her abdomen.

"Not yet," she whispered, but the command was in her whispered words. Her way—he smiled—she was used to having everything her way. He moved his hand down over her abdomen again, and she caught it once more. This time he flung her hand aside, spun her onto her back, and bit down on the full, deep mound.

"Oh," she gasped. "No," she began, but he cut her off with the swift movement of his hand, down into the black wiry bush down farther. She was wet, wanting, but unable to stop having it her way. He moved quickly, pushing her full thighs open and thrusting into her at once, moving quickly, almost harshly. "Oh, Jesus, no . . . oh, God . . ." she half-screamed, protest in her voice, but he felt her thighs fall open wider and her pelvis lift to meet his thrustings.

"You say no?" he murmured against her breasts, pushing faster.

"I . . . oh, Jesus . . . oh . . ." she gasped out as he felt her hands clasping him, pulling at his sides. He rode hard and her body moved to meet his; her breath became a cadenced sound, faster, faster, as he held nothing back. She suddenly twisted, her legs tightening, and the sound from her was deep, a guttural cry that hung in the darkness as he exploded along with her. The cry continued to sound, fading away only when she at last fell back, her breath now short, quick gasps, the aftermath of ecstasy. Her eyes came to focus on him after a moment, blinking slowly.

"You've been spoiled," he said blandly. "Sometimes it's better not to have it your way."

She didn't answer for a long moment. "Maybe," she conceded finally.

"I take it you figure to add this as an extra to the payroll," Fargo said.

Caroline pulled herself to one elbow, nodded. "Be-

20

fore, during, if you want, and after. Whenever you want," she said.

"You've a husband. What about him?" Fargo asked.

"Harry won't be a problem. He hasn't been anything for years," the woman said coldly. "Will you do it? Will you take the job?"

The thousand in gold danced inside Fargo's head. Many men gave a lifetime and got less. He'd need to give only one summer to it. It was too good to turn down. Besides, a summer holed up alone might be a good thing, time to think, to reassess one's life. He turned his eyes back to Caroline Stanton, let his glance move slowly over the full-fleshed beauty of her body.

"If I take it, I do it my way," he said. "No orders, no arguments, not about anything. Understand?" He cupped his hand under one full breast.

"Yes. Your way," she said softly. "No arguments about anything."

He flashed a grin at her. "You learn quick," he said.

"You teach good," she returned.

"Want another lesson?" He slid at her.

Her answer was to reach for him, let a low sigh rise from deep inside her. He let her enjoy herself for a few minutes. There were all kinds of ways to give a lesson.

It was a little before dawn when he stood before her, dressed, ready to leave. She'd finally slipped on a robe in a pretense of modesty. "I want to meet Harry," Fargo told her. "You say you run the show, but the outfit carries his name on it. I want to know for myself that he's going along with this."

"He'll be back tomorrow night," Caroline said.

"I'll be here," Fargo said.

Caroline Stanton pressed against him, her lips on his. "You won't be sorry you took the job, I promise," she murmured. "I'll see to that."

"No, I'll see to that," he corrected. He left her, went outside, and swung onto the pinto to ride away with but a few minutes of night left. In the near distance, the Wind River Mountains rose up to almost blot out the sky, silent, waiting, unmoving. They didn't seem as though they'd welcome still another mountain man.

2

He slept late in the morning, finally woke, and dressed slowly. A cup of coffee downstairs finished the waking up for him, and he climbed onto the pinto and turned the horse to skirt the back side of the town. He let his eyes scan the wooden buildings as he passed the Rocky Mountain Fur Company warehouse and then, a little farther on, he found the name he sought. Two large sheds, neither in good condition, and a smaller structure to one side all were part of a group identified by an almost-illegible name in faded white paint on one side of the first shed: BOWERS FUR TRADING.

Fargo moved toward the structure from the back, swung down from the pinto, and led the horse around to the front of the nearest shed with the door half-open. He peered inside to see one wall of drying and stretching racks and another wall of saddle gear. One splintered long table took up the center of the room. He moved to the adjoining shed and peered inside, found it almost a duplicate of the first one except that the table was more splintered. He felt his eyes narrow as he searched for racks for furs, solid bins, stacks of canvas wrapping cloth. He found only a few wooden dividers leaning against one wall. The sheds were makeshift, clearly not set up to house any

23

large fur traffic for storage and packing. Furs coming through these sheds were quickly sent on their way.

He turned to the smaller structure, where a high window faced one side, the door and another window at the front. He peered into the high side window, saw it was an office with a single battered wood filing cabinet, a swivel chair with a split arm, and a rolltop desk that stood open. He left the pinto and pushed against the door, slipped inside as it swung open at once. One long stride brought him to the file cabinet and he yanked out the top drawer. Yellowed, empty file folders were carelessly scattered in the drawer. The two drawers below held more of the same, just empty file folders.

He turned to the desk, scanned a half-dozen loose papers on the top: supply invoices. In one corner he saw a stack of four-by-four slips of paper, ruffled through them. Each was stamped with the single word RECEIPT in bold type. He stared at the slips for a moment. No name on any of them. No Bowers Fur Trading, no address, nothing but the single word. Strange. Even grubby little freight outfits had their names on their receipts. He pulled open the top drawer of the desk. A ledger book stared back at him, and he flipped the pages open at once. He saw columns of numbers going down the pages, obviously cash amounts, but nothing else, no names, no sellers and no buyers listed, no suppliers and no consignees.

He had just closed the book when he heard the door being opened. He turned to see a girl in the doorway as he pushed the desk drawer shut with his leg. The girl frowned at him, but she had a pert, pretty face, a little turned-up nose, round cheeks, and snapping brown eyes. Short brown hair framed her face and a red-checked shirt, open at the neck, rested on sharply upturned breasts. She wore a gun belt, he saw, with a .38 in the holster.

"What are you doing here?" she demanded.

"Waiting to see somebody," he said.

"What for?" she snapped back.

"Looking for work," he said.

"You're a liar," she said, stepping into the office. "Who are you?"

"Who are *you*?" he returned.

"Sally Bowers," she replied. "You were going through that desk."

"Now, why'd I want to do that?" Fargo said mildly.

Her brown eyes continued to blaze. "Because others have come snooping around here. Caroline Stanton send you?"

"Who's Caroline Stanton?" Fargo asked innocently, watched how her deep angry breathing pushed the twin points sharply into the red-checked shirt.

"You damn well know who she is, I'm thinking," Sally Bowers flung at him. "And I know what she's been saying about my brother."

"What's that mean?" Fargo asked calmly.

"Implications, innuendos, and outright lies, that's what," Sally Bowers retorted. "Her and her loose talk and snooping cowhands." Her hand went to the gun, snapped it out; a damn quick draw, he noted.

"Not bad." Fargo smiled at her.

"Get out," Sally Bowers barked.

Fargo half-shrugged and moved toward the door. She stepped back, but he saw the gun was held straight and steady. "Been working here long with your brother?" he asked.

"No, not that it's any of your business. Go on, get out," Sally Bowers ordered. "Don't come back. Tell Caroline Stanton anyone else she sends will get himself shot."

"I never said she sent me," Fargo remarked casually as he stepped outside. He saw the girl's snapping brown eyes narrow for an instant.

"No, you never did, but that doesn't mean much," she said, following him out.

He paused by the pinto, glanced at the gun in her hand, still pointed levelly toward him. "You know, you shouldn't play with those things. You could hurt somebody," he said.

Her eyes flashed angrily. "I could kill somebody, if I wanted to," she snapped. "I don't play with guns."

Fargo swung onto the pinto, looked down at the girl, took in the sharply upturned breasts, the neat waist that curved into slender hips. Her body went with her face, full of fire and sass. "You're too pretty to get yourself so stirred up." He smiled slowly.

Her eyes met his. "You're too good-looking to get yourself shot," she returned.

He nodded at her, wheeled the pinto around.

"What's your name, mister?" he heard her call out.

He glanced back at her, saw she was holstering the gun. "Don't have one," he said, waved a hand, and rode slowly away. He didn't look back but felt her eyes on him till he was out of sight down the road. The defense of her brother had been no act. The fury in her eyes had been real, and she'd been full of honest anger. He'd seen enough of the false kind to usually spot the difference. But the Bowers operation had a funny smell to it, he decided. No names on anything, not even financial ledgers, receipts, nothing that could be used as evidence or proof of anything, a business run out of the hip pocket. Something was out of order. He felt it inside himself.

He rode on to find a spot under a shade tree, dismounted, and fished a scrap of paper from his shirt pocket. He sat down, made a list on it, and when he'd finished, put the paper back in his pocket and rode back to town in the late-afternoon shadows. He was nearing the Bowers sheds when he pulled up, rode the pinto behind a cluster of elms as he saw Sally Bowers emerge, to mount a chestnut bay in one easy motion. She waited and a man came out of the office, swung onto a black gelding beside her. He had Sally Bowers' brown eyes but without the brightness and fire in them, the same lines as in her face but lengthened, harder, a mouth that turned down at the corners to give his face a hint of selfishness. Craig Bowers was perhaps four or five years older than his sister, Fargo guessed, and the resemblance was strictly on the surface.

He waited till they rode out of sight and then went on into town, retrieved his saddlebag from where he'd left it in the room. It'd be his last visit to the town until the winds of fall sent the leaves swirling. Unless things happened faster than he expected. He then rode out to the Stanton ranch, reached it just as night fell. Caroline Stanton greeted him in riding britches and a velvet jacket. Her blue-gray eyes held a silent smile, which he reckoned she aimed only at him.

"Please come in, Fargo," she said crisply. "Harry's waiting to see you."

He followed her into the house, managed to hold back surprise at the man who rose to greet him. Harry Stanton was at least thirty years older than his wife, a man with a tired face full of waverings.

"This is Skye Fargo," the woman introduced smoothly.

The man's tentative handshake matched his bearing. "Glad you're going to help us," Harry Stanton said. "We'll do whatever you want to put a stop to this thing."

"Get Mr. Fargo a drink, Harry," Caroline ordered.

Fargo watched the man turn to the silver serving cart and get out the glass and the bourbon.

"I was at the Bowers warehouse today," Fargo told the woman.

"Find out anything?" she asked quickly.

"Enough to make me wonder about the operation," he answered. "You could be right about Bowers."

"I am right about Craig Bowers," Caroline snapped.

"I met his sister, Sally," Fargo said.

Caroline Stanton sniffed derisively. "That one. She arrived about a month ago. He supposedly brought her out to tend to the place while he goes on trips. She's in it with him all the way, I'm sure."

Harry Stanton handed the drink to him, and Fargo took it quickly, pulled hard on it. He fished the list

27

from his pocket and handed it to Harry Stanton. He suppressed a grunt as Stanton immediately handed it to Caroline. "Equipment I'll need. I don't want to be seen in town again, especially buying this stuff. You can pick it up easy and without starting any talk," Fargo said.

Caroline looked at the list, smoothed the scrap of paper out, and read aloud. "Six traps, two number-one traps and two number-three. One underwater trap for beaver and muskrat, one heavy bear trap. Staghorn bottle of asafetida, two pairs extra moccasins, a six-inch hunting knife, one eight-inch skinning knife, one hand ax, one broadax, one long-handled hewing ax, one pack mule." She stopped and looked up at him.

"There's a stream at the foot of the mountains, where the road ends. I'll be waiting there at noon tomorrow," Fargo said, finishing his drink.

"It'll be there for you," Caroline said.

He turned to Harry Stanton. The man shook hands with him again.

"We're counting on you, Fargo. You nail Craig Bowers to the wall on this," the man said.

"I'll see you out," Caroline said brusquely, and Fargo followed her outside. "I told you Harry would agree to everything," she said, a little smugly.

"Why'd you marry him?" he asked her as he unhitched the pinto.

"I found out how much money there was in the fur-trading business. He wasn't getting near enough out of it as an agent until I took over," Caroline Stanton said. "And I don't intend to lose it all now to some young swindling crook."

"I guess not, seeing as how it'll all be yours one day," Fargo said.

"I'll have even more to offer then," the woman said.

Fargo allowed her a smile as he swung onto the horse and rode off, to vanish in the night. He picked a spot under a thick sycamore, slept quickly in his bedroll, and woke with the morning sun. He lay back, relaxed, let the sun grow warm and wash over him, and then found himself thinking about Sally Bowers instead of about Caroline. Maybe she had been a damn good little actress. Caroline Stanton was sure she was in it with her brother, and Caroline's suspicions of Craig Bowers seemed pretty damn right. Time would tell. If Craig Bowers was behind the fast swindle operation, and his sister was part of it, he'd find out when the time came. Bowers couldn't just sit back and wait for the mountain men to trickle down from the wild fastness with their bounty. There had to be some contacts made beforehand, some channels set up.

He lay back until the sun rose high, pulled himself up, and rode to where the stream bordered the foot of the mountains. He followed it till it met the end of the road from town. He spotted the laden pack mule under a clump of peachleaf willows and headed toward it. He'd just reached it when a figure stepped from beneath the trees. "I decided to bring it myself," Caroline Stanton said as he dismounted, peered under the canvas-covered pack. "It's all there, everything you ordered and an extra tarpaulin," she said.

"Good," he grunted, turned to her, and found her arms sliding around his neck, her lips pressing hard against his mouth.

"Just so you'll remember," she said, pulling away after a long moment.

"I've a damn good memory," Fargo said.

"After the other night, I'm wondering if I can go the whole summer," Caroline said.

"Just keep thinking of getting all those furs to sell again," he said.

She shrugged, but the blue-gray eyes hardened. "I'll do that," she said. "You're a hard man, Fargo."

"That's why I'm here, isn't it?" he asked, and her lips grew tight, the answer needing no words. He took the reins of the mule, swung into the saddle, nodded to Caroline Stanton, and started to move forward. He didn't look back. His eyes stayed on the wall of green that frowned down on him, and in a matter of minutes he was starting to climb the first slopes of the Wind River Mountains.

By late afternoon he'd traveled a good ways up into the heavy tree cover of the mountains. He'd set an order of priorities for himself to cover the first weeks. Finding a good spot was number one. The second was shelter. He'd need a cabin. Even in the summer, the nights grew chill and the thunderstorms could soak a man to death. A cabin was a must, though he'd not spend time on anything fancy and hewed to a tight fit. He'd not be spending the winter, when a proper squared-log, mud-packed cabin would be a necessity. Third was to get his traps out, and fourth to make the land as familiar as the back of his hand.

The first task, finding a good spot, proved to be the easiest. Almost anywhere was a good place, he realized as he traveled higher into the fastness of the mountains. The land ran with a thousand sparkling mountain streams and was alive with game, for both trapping and eating. On this first afternoon he'd caught sight of mule deer, raccoon, possum, grouse and pheasant, red fox, lynx, black bear, and every kind of hare. The rest of the game, he knew, was waiting in hollows and logs, watery dens and leafy bowers.

He kept climbing until night fell, slept in his bedroll, and chewed some hardtack; and with the new dawn he was climbing again. He paused at a level place and saw a wisp of smoke in the distance from a mountain man's cabin. He kept going, turned to the left to level off his progress, and moved in and out of forested hollows and slopes, searching until he found a spot with a good stand of white oak. He put everything else aside for a solid week and worked from sunup to sundown, first chopping trees down, then scoring the logs, and after that squaring the timber with the hewing ax.

He cut most everything he needed first, including the treenails, before starting to build, and so the building of the cabin itself went fast. He didn't open too much land, taking care that the shallow-rooted trees wouldn't be thrown down by windstorms or leave the hardwoods to rush out new shoots to grab all the new sunlight. Some trees were like some people, pushy and aggressive. When he was finished, the small cabin fitted tightly enough for the summer, and he didn't bother to mud-calk the logs. He rested most of one day, and the next morning he began to set his line of traps. A broad swift-running mountain stream was plenty deep enough for one trap, and he found a small lake full of beaver and muskrat. He grimaced with every trap he set, taking consolation from the fact that the mountains teemed with every kind of wildlife and some badly in need of thinning out before winter.

Within another week, the days had taken on a routine and an order, and he had time to ride and explore the mountain fastness. He ranged a good distance and saw signs of other mountain men, snares, traps, and through distant trees, a curl of smoke. He saw signs of wolf, too, and one afternoon he glimpsed a powerful grizzly in the distance; automatically, he touched at the curved bear scar on his forearm. The shoeless hooves of Indian ponies caught his eye also, and he found an Arapaho gauntlet half-hidden under a rotted log. He put a stout wooden bolt on the cabin door that night. Danger and beauty, death and life, walked hand in hand in the richness of the Wind River Mountains.

That truth exploded in front of him but a few mornings later. He'd just emptied two traps and tied a small bundle of red-fox skins together when he heard the sound of a horse racing through the thick brush of the slope. Fargo's eyes went to the pinto at once; he saw the horse well back of a thick clump of oak and he dropped flat on the ground. In moments, the horseman came into view, a young Indian boy, not more than twelve, fear on his face as, bent low over the horse's back, he raced recklessly through the heavy foliage. He wore but a breechcloth and a head-band, but the headband bore the beadwork of the Poncas.

Frowning, Fargo lifted his head as the boy disap-peared into the trees, as though racing wildly away from something. The answer came a moment later as Fargo saw the horsemen, three riding down the far ridge, two more circling around in back of where he lay hidden. Arapaho, he thought, five young bucks. Six, he corrected as the last one came roaring down on the fleeing boy's tracks. The Indian rode with lips pulled back, his face harsh, an ugly scar running down one side of his forehead.

Fargo rose as the Arapaho rode on. He didn't give the boy much chance. He wasn't the rider the young bucks were, but more to the point, the Poncas weren't the killer-warriors the Arapaho were. They fought when they had to fight, but they were basically a peaceful group with none of the warlike qualities of their cousins, the Sioux. Fargo walked to where the pinto waited, swung into the saddle, and started on the trail of the pursuers. Curiosity, he told himself, but he knew better. He never liked an uneven fight, even among Indians, particularly one this uneven, with a slip of a boy against six bloodthirsty Arapaho bucks. It wasn't the way of things for a white man to intrude into Indian tribal fights, but since he was one-quarter Cherokee, Fargo figured he had a better excuse than most.

He caught up to the sound of the racing horses, slowed, followed more carefully, and then, suddenly, a piercing cry shattered the forest. It was the young boy's voice. Fargo spurred the pinto on, crested the top of the slope, leaped down to the ground, left the horse, and crawled on foot to where he could glimpse the Arapaho ponies. He came up behind them and dropped to one knee. The Arapaho had the boy, two of them holding him by the arms, and he saw the boy's face already bloodied on one side. As he watched, the buck with the scar on his forehead yanked the breechcloth from the boy. He pointed to the boy's penis, laughed coarsely, reached out, and pulled hard at the young organ. The boy cried out in pain. The buck punched him in the belly and the boy doubled over, fell as the other bucks let him go. The scarred one said something Fargo didn't catch, but the meaning became clear instantly as one of the others pulled a hatchet from his waist and brought it down with all his strength on the boy's calf. Fargo heard the crack of bone and the boy screamed again, flipped onto his back in anguish.

The one with the scar barked orders again and two of the others pinned the boy's arms down to the ground. The one who was obviously the leader moved to the boy, now spread-eagled on the ground. Again, he ran his hands over the boy's penis, then drew a hunting knife from a sheath. Grinning, he knelt down, lifted the boy's testicles, and began to bring the knife closer. Eyes wide with terror, the boy screamed again and again.

Fargo's eyes bored into the Arapaho's face as the man brought the knife up to the boy's organ, saw the Indian's lips pull back in cruel pleasure. It was no exercise in terror. The buck intended to carry it through. Fargo snapped the big Colt .45 into his hand, aimed, and fired in a split second. The Arapaho's body jerked upward, then pitched forward half over the boy, the knife falling from his hand. Fargo fired again, two shots fired so quickly they sounded almost as one. One of the Arapaho holding the boy's arms fell back, his forehead gushing red. Another buck, standing next to him, half-spun, his hands grabbing at his abdomen, turning deep red at once. He dropped to his knees first, then collapsed on his side.

Fargo held back a fourth shot as the other three dived in all directions, rolling and twisting, disappearing into the brush. He slid back down the top of the slope, found a dense thicket, and pushed himself into it. He adjusted his grip on the gun, keeping one finger on the trigger. They would come looking for him. They had to find him. Or die in the process. Running back to their camp without his scalp was out of the question. If they weren't simply killed or banished, they'd be sent to live with the squaws and there was only one answer to that for an Arapaho brave. They had to come for him.

But they wouldn't come crashing through the brush. This time they'd use every bit of hunting skill. And one thing more. Their noses. They'd smell him out sooner or later, move in on the smell of leather and white man's sweat. He had only to wait and watch and know how the trapped hare feels.

His ears picked up the rustle of leaves, the sound growing louder. The ponies were being moved, and Fargo stayed hunched in the thicket, peered through the leaves for a glimpse of figures. Silence, except for the soft, pain-filled gasps of the boy just beyond the top of the slope. They wouldn't rush. They had time, but he wondered why they had moved the ponies. A flash of copper skin along the top of the ridge afforded part of the answer, moving too quickly for a shot. They wanted the slope cleared. The rest of the answer came moments later as the first arrow thudded into the tree just to his left. They'd found his hiding spot. He flattened himself on the ground as three other arrows slashed into the thicket. Two buried their warheads into the earth less than an inch from him, the third one brushing the top of his hair as it shot past.

A pause followed, and Fargo stayed flattened. The second flurry of arrows came to slam into the thicket. This time he let out a guttural groan, cut it off in the middle with a choking gasp. He had only a moment to wait. The first brave rose up, running, leaping down the slope toward the thicket, a grin on his face, the bow in one hand. Fargo saw the other two appear, start after him. He rose, fired point-blank at

34

the first Arapaho almost at the thicket. "Don't believe everything you hear," Fargo muttered as the shot exploded.

The Arapaho halted as though struck by a mule, staggered back, stomach torn open. Fargo's second shot caught the following Arapaho in the chest, sent him toppling sideways. But the third Indian catapulted himself down in a leaping dive before the second brave's body struck the ground. Fargo brought his gun up again, but the Indian was on him, his shot going wild. He felt himself flung backwards onto the ground. His elbow hit a rock and instantly the pain and numbness went through his forearm. He felt the gun fall from his fingers as he tried to twist away. The Arapaho got an arm around his neck and Fargo fell backward again as the Indian pulled. He let himself go with the pull and the Indian fell back off balance. His right arm hanging numbly, Fargo flung himself in a twisting arc, dislodged the Indian's grip as he fell to one knee. He swept out with his left arm, caught the Arapaho back of the knees, and saw the man flip over backward.

Fargo rolled away as the Indian regained his feet, cursing silently at the numb helplessness of his right arm. The Arapaho came at him and Fargo saw the flash of the hunting knife in the man's hand. He moved backward as the Indian swept the blade at him in wide, slashing arcs. He kept going back, and the Arapaho grew bold at once. He leaped forward with a vicious thrust. Fargo felt the blade graze his arm as he dropped to his knees. The Indian's body struck him as the man fell forward, and Fargo straightened up, uncurling powerful leg muscles to send the Arapaho flipping over his shoulders. He whirled as the brave struck the ground, kicked out with his leg in a blow that caught the Arapaho on the side of the head. The Indian fell sideways, but still clutched the knife in his hand. Fargo arced a looping left that caught the Arapaho at the point of the jaw. The brave's head snapped back and this time

35

the knife fell from his hand. Fargo kicked it away, scooped it up with his left hand, and the Arapaho dived at his legs. Fargo met the dive with an upward sweep of the blade. He felt it go through the tendons of the lower neck and a cascade of warm liquid showered his hand. He leaped to the side and the Arapaho pitched on his face in front of him, to lay motionless. A circle of deep red oozed from beneath the man's head to stain the ground.

Fargo dropped back another pace, moved his right arm. Slowly, the numbness was lessening, a tingling returning to his forearm. He flexed the arm and massaged the elbow as he retrieved the Colt, put it in its holster, and made his way to the top of the slope. The Indian boy had crawled a half-dozen yards and lay with his face contorted with pain, one leg drawn up. Fargo went to him, knelt down, and saw the gratitude in the boy's eyes was mixed with fear. He drew upon the Dakota tongue he knew. "It is over," he said. "You are safe."

He looked at the leg. The break had swollen tissues and the skin bled. Fargo rose, retrieved the pinto, and brought the boy's pony back to him. "Can you ride?" he asked. "It will hurt." Pride fought its way into the boy's pain-filled face. He started to rise, almost fell, and Fargo caught him, lifted him onto the horse. He helped the boy swing the broken leg over the pony's back, watched as the boy took a deep breath and straightened his slim, slender body.

"I am ready," the boy said. "Where do you take me?"

"You lead the way to your people," Fargo said.

The boy's eyes widened in surprise and he nodded gravely, turned the pony to move diagonally across the face of the mountain. Fargo swung in beside him and they rode in silence until Fargo halted for a moment. "Do you want rest?" he asked.

The boy shook his head, but Fargo saw the slender jaw twitch. The boy spurred the pony on and Fargo followed. They had gone another five miles, moving downward on the mountain, and Fargo was beginning to wonder if he'd best turn back when the tops of the tepees came into view. Half a dozen riders appeared at once, came toward him, lances in hand. They parted to each side, and Fargo followed the boy's pony into the camp. The boy halted and a tall Indian wearing a chief's headdress emerged from a gray-white tepee, his impassive face unable to hide concern. At a gesture, two young bucks took the boy from the saddle, carried him to the chief, laid him on the ground.

Fargo stayed in the saddle, his eyes flicking around the crowd that had gathered at once. He could feel an edge of hostility, but only an edge, and the chief knelt down beside the boy. Fargo could catch some of the boy's words as he began to talk through his pain, excitement in his voice. Obviously, the boy was the chief's son, and finally the man rose, motioned for Fargo to dismount. Fargo swung down from the pinto, saw that the Indian chief was perhaps a half-head taller than he.

"My son has told me what happened," the chief said in English, saw the surprise in Fargo's eyes. "I learned your tongue from traders and trappers. You saved my son's life."

"Didn't like the odds," Fargo said.

"Many would have run the other way," the chief said. "I am Tantowa, chief of the Poncas here. My son rode out too far alone. But for you, he would be dead now. He tells that you killed six Arapaho by yourself."

"I was lucky," Fargo said.

The Ponca chief smiled with his eyes. "No, it was my son who had luck because you were near. What do they call you?"

"Fargo," the Trailsman answered.

"Fargo," the Ponca chief repeated slowly. "We will call you the one who saves. Are you a mountain man?"

"Only for this summer," Fargo told him.

"You are here in the mountains by yourself?" the chief asked, and Fargo nodded. Tantowa turned to a young buck, spoke quickly in the Ponca dialect Fargo failed to catch, and the buck moved quickly away. The chief looked down at his son as two old squaws came with skins soaked in something. They pressed the skins around the break in the boy's leg and Fargo smelled the unmistakable odor of comfrey, the plant known to promote healing of broken bones and bruises.

"You have given my son's life to him and to me," Tantowa said. Fargo turned again to the chief. "Such a gift will take much to repay. Until I can find such a time, I give a gift to help you, mountain man."

Tantowa gestured, and Fargo looked past him at the girl being brought by the young buck. His eyes held on the striking beauty of her face, even-featured, almost classic, eyes of a doe, deep and liquid brown, her hair worn long in two braids. She wore a deerskin skirt and a vest, open at the front except for one thong in the center. Her breasts, coppery mounds, rose up from the edges of the vest, full and high. She halted in front of him, and he saw her eyes flick over his frame with instant appraisal, but they revealed nothing more.

"This is Suni," the chief said. "A maiden of our tribe as yet untouched. She is yours, mountain man."

Fargo's thoughts raced. The gesture was one of gratitude and friendship. To refuse it would be an insult. Yet he didn't want an Indian girl dogging his heels, even one as lovely as this. "You may, according to our custom, keep her as your woman or take her as your wife," the chief went on. "Or you may enjoy her and return her if that is your wish."

Another thought pushed its way forward in Fargo's racing mind. Mountain men often took squaw wives to cook and sew for them. Sooner or later, he'd have visitors coming to look and hopefully tip their hand in time. The girl might be perfect to complete his role

38

in their eyes. "A pony goes with her," he heard Tantowa say as the chief saw his hesitation.

"You honor me by such a gift," Fargo said. "I shall take the girl with me."

"A small gift compared to my son's life. You will be welcome here, always, Fargo," the Indian chief said. Fargo exchanged the sign of friendship with the chief and swung himself onto the pinto. He watched as a squaw gave the girl a blanket and a large parfleche. A young brave brought a bay-colored pony to her and she pulled herself onto the bare back of the horse. Her deep copper-cream breasts flashed openly for an instant, beautiful as a tanager bursting from the brush. Fargo held his hand upraised, palm out to the chief and the others as he wheeled the pinto around. He rode slowly from the camp, through a line of Ponca braves and squaws, aware the girl was on the pony just behind him. He didn't look back. It was not expected and he led the way back across the face of the mountain, climbing higher as the day neared an end. He grimaced as he saw the dusk begin to lower with too much speed and motioned for the girl to ride beside him. She spurred her pony forward and came alongside him.

He watched her breasts sway with the motion of the horse. She rode easily, as if she and the pony were one. Her profile remained unsmiling, eyes fixed on the path ahead. He sought for words, drew upon his halting Sioux. "Do not be afraid, Suni," he offered.

She turned her face to him for a moment. The liquid doe's eyes were impassive, but they certainly held no fear. "I do not fear," she said.

"Do you know my tongue?" he asked, sure his Sioux would not hold up for everyday conversation.

"A little," she said in English. "I can learn more."

"My name is Fargo," he told her.

She nodded gravely, returned her eyes to the path.

Damn, it was almost dark, he noted. Night would be on them long before they reached the cabin, and he felt uneasy. His right forearm still had spurts of numbness and he didn't know these mountains well enough yet to wrestle with the night. He quickened the pace and she stayed with him easily. The night almost on them, he spotted a passageway under a low rock ledge. He motioned to it, set off at a fast canter. Riding too fast, he started under the low ledge of flat rock. He never saw the cougar until it screamed and leaped in one lightninglike motion. The tawny form flashed over him and the pinto exploded in fear, reared up, and bucked all at one instant. Fargo felt himself thrown sideways. A tree branch caught him alongside the head, snapping his neck around, but he retained presence of mind enough to throw his arms in front of him as he hit the ground. The world fell away, became a gray curtain as he lay on the ground. He pulled himself up on one elbow, shook his head. The gray curtain lifted and the dark green of the forest returned.

The cougar screamed again and Fargo heard the girl's voice cry out in fright. He fought his eyes to stay clear, focus enough to see the long tawny shape crouching to spring again. His vision began to fog once more as he yanked the Colt from the holster. He shook his head, saw only a dim tawny blur. He fired off three shots through a haze, knew he was firing wildly. He shook his head, and his vision cleared enough for him to see the cougar disappearing into the trees.

Fargo fell on one knee as the world started to spin again. He felt the girl beside him, shook his head hard until his eyes cleared again, and he saw her beside him, a frown of concern on the smooth bronze brow. "*Damn*, my fault," he muttered. "Hurrying like a damn schoolboy."

The accusation was accurate. He'd been in too much of a hurry, plowing under a rock ledge without even a glance up to it. His head hurt and he saw the haze moving into his eyes again. He rose, cleared his vision, saw that the Indian girl had hold of him with both hands. He looked away, whistled for the pinto, whistled three more times. Finally the horse came into sight, moved toward him. He started for the horse, realized Suni was still helping to support him. He reached the pinto and pulled himself into the saddle, sat there for a moment, and felt himself swaying. He forced himself to stay straight and knew that the dimness wasn't all in his eyes. The last light was barely clinging to the top of the trees and he started forward again. He caught Suni's glance of concern.

"I'll be all right," he said, and managed a smile. It was an effort. His head pounded. She returned a grave, unsmiling nod. He spurred the pinto on and went up the only path he saw. It grew steeper quickly, but the girl stayed close behind, he saw. Damn, his head throbbed and pounded, he thought. They were moving up higher into the mountains, definitely the direction he wanted to go. They rode in almost-absolute blackness now, and branches reached out to catch at him. Through the pounding of his head he saw the girl beside him and he forced himself to keep on. When the dizziness caught up to him again and the pounding in his head only worsened, he halted, peered into the night, and cursed the pain inside him.

"You are lost," he heard the girl say. "Lost and in pain."

His lips pressed together in admittance. "There's a stream somewhere. If I can find it, I'll be all right."

"Stream? I hear a stream," the girl said. "This way."

She moved forward and Fargo followed, the pounding in his head continuing. They were at the stream before he heard the sound of it, and this time he led the way again, moving along the edge of the water, climbing up higher. They traveled another hour at least, he guessed, when the stream was joined by a second, smaller rivulet. He turned, followed the second stream, which led upward at a more gentle climb, cutting west along the heavily wooded mountainside. His head felt as though it were about to fall off, and his neck and shoulder muscles were aflame.

He continued on, fighting off waves of dizziness, and a high moon filtered weak silver light through the forest, enough to make riding a little less precarious. He'd lost track of time—Suni riding beside him, glancing at him with concern—when the cabin finally took shape through the trees. He rode almost to the door, slid from the pinto, and rested his forehead against the horse's forequarter for a moment. The girl dismounted, and he pointed to the small covered lean-to he had built alongside the cabin. She led the pinto and her own pony into the shelter, unsaddled the pinto as Fargo went into the cabin. He sank down onto the blankets on the floor, shivering suddenly with the chill night air. Eyes closed, he lay still and tried to lessen the throbbing of his head. Slowly, he became aware of warmth, opened one eye to see that the girl had lighted a fire. He closed his eye and a few moments later felt her hand on his forehead, stroking gently. He felt wetness, a soft pressure. She was putting warm cloths on his head. "Sleep," he heard her say. "Sleep."

He made no protest. The pounding had become a dull ache that felt better with his eyes closed and head back. He was fighting a concussion, he was certain. Dimly, he heard the girl moving about the room, closing the door of the cabin, and then sleep swept all else away with its blanket of silence.

He slept heavily but woke in the deep of the night, lay unmoving, letting his thoughts pull themselves together. His head had stopped pounding and he moved his right arm. The numbness had gone entirely and he pulled himself up on one elbow. Shoulder and neck muscles still ached. He glanced around, found the girl asleep, wrapped in a large Indian blanket. She lay close to the fire, now hardly more than embers. He lay back down and let sleep flow over him once again.

3

It was morning when he woke again, the sun's warmth coming into the cabin through the open door. He sat up, saw that he was alone in the cabin. The Indian blanket lay neatly folded and placed in a corner of the room. He got up, went to the bucket of cold water he kept inside the cabin, and washed quickly. The water banished all vestiges of sleep at once.

He felt good, his head clear and the ache in his upper torso only a reminder of how close he had come to a broken neck. He dressed and went outside, blinked in the brightness of the morning sun. The bushes moved and he saw the girl appear. She had been at the stream, her hair wet, little drops of stream water glistening on her face and neck. She had put on a deerskin dress that hung loosely, but her breasts, swaying beneath the garment, moved it provocatively. She halted before him and her soft doe eyes searched his face.

"You are good," she said after a moment.

"Yes, fine," he said, and the hint of a frown touched her face. He moved his arms. "I'm all right now."

She nodded, started to move past him, and he reached out to touch her arm. She halted at once.

"Thank you," he said, "for last night."

She nodded again. He smiled at her, but she didn't return the smile, her lovely features unmoving, touched with a gravity that was neither hostile nor welcoming. He took his hand from her arm and followed her into the cabin. She halted, looked at the provisions he had on the single shelf he'd put up; a bag of coffee, a store of sourdough he'd made and put in a jar. A little frown slid over her face.

"I'll make breakfast," he told her, and she looked quizzically at him. "Eat," he said in Sioux, and pointed to himself. She nodded, unsmiling.

He took some of the sourdough, added molasses, and mixed it well together, used the griddle pan from his saddlebag. He cooked up his version of johnnycakes as the girl watched, her eyes taking in his every move. "Johnnycakes," he told her, pointed to the little mounds in the griddle pan. He repeated the word, and she nodded. He decided she wasn't ready to learn that the word was a bastardization, that they'd originally been called journey cakes. He brewed coffee, handed her a mug. "Drink," he told her, and she sniffed first, hounddog fashion, then sipped it cautiously. She paused, savored it, sipped again, a larger sip, and finally nodded her head in approval. He smiled at her and she looked back with her liquid doe's eyes over the rim of the mug. He wondered if she ever smiled as he dug into his johnnycakes.

When they finished breakfast, he set out to see to his traps. Suni went with him and he saw that she had a hunting knife strapped to the thong at the waistline of the one-piece deerskin dress. He spent the day emptying and resetting the traps, moving along the trap line from one to the other; by the day's end, he found some of the first ones full again. Game was bountiful in the early summer days of the thickly forested mountains. The girl was a real help. She knew how to skin and lay out furs to dry and how to roll those that needed rolling. They rested at midday and he taught her English words for everyday objects.

She, in turn, told him the Ponca dialect for the same things. She listened gravely, nodding often, eager to learn and to practice.

"Beautiful," he said to her when they'd finished the midday rest, and she frowned at him. He laughed, pointed to a cluster of black-eyed Susans, picked one, and held it up. "Beautiful," he repeated, making the Sioux sign for worship. She nodded in understanding. "You are beautiful," he told her. The soft doe eyes held his gaze and she nodded again. But she didn't smile.

When the day ended, they brought back a full catch of pelts, plenty of marten, beaver, red fox, and possum with a good bit of hare. Suni cut the meat from the hares and wrapped it in leaves, brought it back to the cabin, where she began to cook it for dinner. He showed her the advantages of an iron kettle and she quickly adapted to using the utensil.

She gathered silverweed root and amaranth and added them to the kettle, stirred, and watched her cooking as Fargo tended to thoroughly cleaning the pelts they had brought back. When he finished, he stretched out to watch her as she moved about the tasks with easy grace. The classic loveliness of her features were highlighted by the play of the firelight, and when she knelt before the fire, it was with a catlike composure, hands on her knees, body somehow neatly folded together. When the hare was ready to eat, he added salt and pepper and she watched with interest, wide-eyed. He stirred the seasoning into the kettle, offered her a taste of the results with the big wooden spoon. She nodded approval and he swung the heavy iron kettle from the fire and dished out the meal. He'd fashioned trenchers and gave her one, took one for himself. She examined it curiously, watched him fill it and then use the knife and two-pronged fork. She was using the fork in minutes as though she'd used it all her life.

The hare was good, tender and tasty with the wild greens she had added to the pot, and Fargo ate hungrily. When they'd finished, she insisted on cleaning the utensils and he went outside to stand under a sky of deep blue velvet scattered with diamond chips. The night had grown cool as it always did this high in the mountains. He heard a cougar scream and, in the far distance, the baying of wolves. The mountains never slept. He saw smoke thicken from the top of the stone chimney he'd built. Suni had put more wood on the fire. The wind speared at him and he opened the cabin door, went back inside.

He halted, felt his breath draw in sharply. Suni looked up from in front of the fire. She had dropped the top of the deerskin dress to her waist and she rose as he entered, faced him, slowly moved toward him. His eyes stayed riveted at the beauty of her, the firelight giving her skin the glow of burnished copper in the sun. Her deep full breasts seemed to shimmer with large areolas of deep copper hue, the nipples flat, almost indented. Her liquid eyes swam with new depths as she halted in front of him. He put his hands on the bare shoulders, felt the smoothness of her skin, looked into the unsmiling face that stared up at him.

"You do not need to do this," he said slowly, shaking his head at her.

"Tantowa gave me to you," she said simply.

"Yes, but you are free. You can do what you want," Fargo said.

"You do not like me?" Suni said. "You called me your word . . . beautiful."

"You *are* beautiful."

"That is not enough?" she asked seriously.

"It is enough, but you do not have to give yourself. Do you understand?" he asked. "You are a free woman."

A small frown furrowed her brow. "Maybe," she said. "But I want to give. It is why Tantowa gave me to you. I want to please you."

"Do you, Suni?" he asked sternly.

46

She nodded slowly, unsmiling, the deep liquid eyes staying on him. "Yes," she said in Sioux.

He felt his hands drop down from her shoulders, watched as she pushed the rest of the deerskin dress down and stepped out of it, to stand naked before him. His eyes moved down her, taking in the beautifully molded legs, the full-hipped torso, and the smooth, flat abdomen. Below the contours of her abdomen almost no nap at all, only a few soft strands. He began to unbutton his shirt, unsnap his belt, but her hands halted his. "Suni do," she murmured. Slowly, she began to undress him, first his shirt, opening each button with careful deliberation. She pulled the belt buckle open, the buttons of his trousers, returned to take the shirt from him. She ran her hands across the hardness of his chest, the sinewy arms, and he saw her eyes glow with tiny lights. Her hands went to his trousers, undid the last button, slid them down his legs with his shorts. He stepped out of the trousers, and she dropped to her knees, cupped both hands around his eager organ, and began to caress, stroking slowly, holding it against her cheeks. He put his hands down to circle her head as she rubbed her face against his penis, then opening her lips, kissed him, drew little caresses with her mouth.

She played with gentleness, and soft sounds came from her, sounds of pleasure and enjoyment. He felt his wanting surging forward, almost exploding when she bent backward, dropping her hands to her sides, offering her cream-copper breasts. He dropped down to her and took first one, then the other in his mouth and felt her legs close around him at once. She pushed upward for him, finding him, easing herself around him with moist warmth.

She moved with him at once, a mounting rhythm that became its own caress. Little sounds came from her, soft cooing calls, and he caught a Sioux word he did not know. But it mattered little, the meaning clear. He thrust into her and she rose to match his every thrust, and suddenly he felt her legs harden

47

around him, her hands grip his shoulders. He let his own surging desire burst with her and suddenly the little screams were replaced by utter silence. Eyes closed, lips drawn back, she continued to pump upward and the silence became its own cry of ecstasy as the moment held, clung, and then, too suddenly, began to fall away. The skyrockets vanished, and he let his body come down slowly upon hers, staying inside her as she breathed deeply and her eyes remained tightly closed.

He lay upon the velvet softness of the copper skin, the soft breasts pushing into his chest. He watched her face, saw her eyes open finally, deep, dark ovals that stared at him. Slowly, he pulled from her, lay down beside her, and she pushed his head against her breasts. He lay there for a moment, rose on one elbow to look down at her. She was smiling, a little catlike smile that almost purred.

"You can smile," he told her.

The smile broadened a fraction and her arms crept around his neck. "Good?" she whispered. "Suni please you?"

"Damn good," Fargo said.

"More?" she said, arms clinging to him.

"Why not?" he answered, pressed down upon her round copper-cream breasts. She arched her back, pushed up against him. His hand went down the smooth skin to the fleshy little pubic mound, so smooth and virtually hairless, a deliciously different sensation to it. He rubbed gently and she lifted her legs up as a flower unfolds its petals, half-turned to push up against his hand. Once again, she closed her eyes as he caressed her and only the tiny tremors of her thighs gave evidence of the pleasure that coursed through her. Once again, when the moment spiraled, her eyes stayed closed and her silence was accented by the fervid thrustings of her hips. There was one difference this time. She smiled, that soft catlike smile, as he throbbed inside her, and when it was over, she curled up beside him, knees drawn up, pulling the large Indian blanket over the both of them. She slept at once, like a satisfied, well-fed cat.

He joined her in sleep after a spell and woke only when the day pushed its way through the slits in the cabin. She woke when he did and her hand slid down to caress him at once. He pressed his hand over hers, gently took her fingers away.

"After," he said. "There is work to do now."

The little catlike smile came. "After," she echoed. He grinned back at her as she flung the blanket off, ran from the cabin in her cream-bronze lovely nakedness. He washed and dressed, using the water he'd fetched in the bucket the day before. When she returned from the stream, he was in the doorway, waiting. She gleamed with hundreds of little water beads on the coppery skin caught by the morning sunlight. Her deep breasts shimmered with bronzed light as she walked.

"Beautiful," he murmured as she brushed past him, her hand lifting to touch his cheek. She slipped the deerskin dress on and followed him to the trap line. This time he took the big Henry .44 carbine, and when they'd emptied all the traps by the day's end, he brought down a mule deer for venison. Suni skinned the deer and hung the venison in strips to dry and age. They brought it in when the night came or they'd not find it by morning.

The days began to weave a pattern and flowed into weeks. Suni was expert at skinning and drying the pelts. By day she was an efficient, happy helper, and by night a continuing source of desire. There were no pretensions on her part, and in the nights her lovemaking was as pure and natural as that of any animal in the forest. And as intense, the wanting simply a basic part of her no more to be denied than to deny satisfying one's hunger or thirst. And when it was done with, she curled into a little ball beside him and slept. None of the playful, warm pleasures of afterward for her. The hunger satisfied, there was no need for more. The smile that had finally come to her lips came quickly and often now, and one night as she stroked her hands along his thighs, cupping his organ and pressing it to her, she turned the deep liquid eyes on him.

"Fargo good. Fargo mine," she murmured.

He stroked the long strands of ebony hair and said nothing. Later, lying awake, he thought about the moment. She had turned what he'd expected to be a long and lonely summer into a time of absolute pleasure, and she was more anxious to please him with each passing day. He'd never heard an Indian word for love and he wondered if there was one. Certainly not in the sense the white man used the word, filled with complicated feelings and surrounded by man-made concepts of morality, good and bad, and proper behavior. Suni's feelings had none of those complications, he was certain. But caring, that was something else, and that existed anywhere and anyplace; and it was damn obvious that she cared very much to be his.

He pushed the idle thoughts away finally. No sense in poking too deep, he told himself. It destroyed enjoyment and he sure as hell didn't want to do that. He grunted, turned on his side, her soft rear warm against his belly, and slept.

But the question refused to vanish. It was a few weeks later, when Suni had just finished making dinner, that he found her outside, eyes on fast-moving clouds as they scudded by. He put his arms around her, pressed the softness of her breasts.

"Too soon," he heard her murmur.

"What is too soon?" he asked.

"The end of the good days," she said. "The white ground coming."

"Winter," he told her, repeated it for her.

"Winter," she echoed, turned, and circled his neck with her arms. Her smile held mischievousness suddenly. "Longer nights for Fargo and Suni," she said.

He went back into the cabin with her, sat down on the floor with her in front of him. "I'm no mountain

50

man, Suni," he said. "When the long nights come, I must leave here."

"Leave mountains?" She frowned, using her hands in a kind of halfway sign language.

"Yes. Leave mountains." He nodded.

She frowned in thought for a long moment, then her shoulders lifted in a little shrug. "Suni go wherever Fargo go," she said simply, drew him to her, opened her mouth on his. He decided to pursue it another time.

The weeks continued to shower game on him and the little cabin was growing crowded with pelts. He had taken to setting traps only every other day to give Suni and himself the time to properly dry and stretch the furs in the sun. It was becoming a definite two-person task. It was late afternoon one sun-swept warm day when the riders appeared. Suni had just taken the pelts down from the drying rack when he saw the horsemen approaching through the trees: four of them riding single file. His hand went to the butt of the big Colt .45, habit more than alarm. He moved toward the cabin door, positioned himself for any sudden moves that might be needed. Suni, a half-dozen red-fox pelts in her arms, halted at the cabin as the men rode up.

The first one wore a dusty tan hat that cast a shadow over a face with a week's stubble on it. He had narrow eyes that refused to smile when his mouth made the effort. "Howdy," the man said.

Fargo nodded, sized up the other three. Worn outfits, the edge of seediness in each of them. Nondescript cowhands on nondescript horses.

"Just passing through," the first man said. "Jed Silver's the name."

"Don't get folks passing through these mountains," Fargo said evenly.

"Doin' some survey work for the government," the man said. "Pass this way a good bit." His eyes went to the stack of furs on the ground by the racks, then to

51

Suni holding the red fox. "Nice set of pelts. You a mountain man?" he said.

Fargo nodded slowly, watched the man's eyes dart to Suni again in a low glance, take in the girl, the long black braids, the high-cheekboned face, the obvious Indian of her.

"You sell to Rocky Mountain Fur Company?" the man asked.

"Yep," Fargo answered.

The man exchanged a fast glance with the other three, tried another smile. His eyes stayed hard. "Good hunting, mountain man," he said. "We'll be passing this way again come end of summer. Maybe we'll see you then."

"Maybe," Fargo agreed blandly. The man waved a hand back at him as he turned his horse to the right, started down a narrow pathway. The other three followed, silent as ghosts. Fargo's eyes held for a moment on each rider as he passed on to disappear down the trail. He waited till they'd vanished into the thick mountain forest. No surveyors, he grunted silently, not that seedy quartet. None of them carried so much as a telescope or a surveyor's tripod, not even a pack mule of provisions tagging along. They weren't spending weeks up in the mountains surveying. They were the first contact, he pondered, his eyes narrowing, advance runners scouting the mountain men, getting a line on whatever they could. Suni being there had helped the picture, just as he'd expected. He turned to the cabin with an armful of the pelts, allowed himself a moment of satisfaction. The rats were sniffing at the bait. Now to find out whose rats.

"Bad men," Suni said as he put the pelts down in the cabin, and he looked at her in surprise.

"Why?" he asked. "You know them?"

"No," she said. "Bad eyes," she added simply.

He smiled, pulled her against him, held her there. The instincts of the wild creatures, he thought, so far sharper than those dulled by civilization. Suni was one of the wild creatures, a child of a heritage of nature's wilderness, all her sensuous, womanly wanting no contradiction, all her sweetness no lie. She proved it again when the night came to cloak the cabin, wanting and sensitivity, primitive passion and the purity of the senses all mixed up together and, afterward, the simple satisfactions.

In the morning, he saw to his trap lines as usual. The next few days were quietly usual, part of the simple pattern that had developed. But he had taken to tending the trap lines alone and leaving Suni to work on the pelts. There were more than enough to keep her busy. The really experienced mountain men must bring a fortune down each fall, he realized. No wonder Caroline was so upset about the business being stolen. The stakes were higher than he'd realized. It was one of those cloudy mornings when the sky kept threatening rain but didn't deliver. He'd set aside two beaver pelts and a muskrat from the lake trap, was just tying them into a bundle when he heard the twig snap. He whirled, gun in hand, saw the huge figure standing with one foot in the stream.

The man carried no gun and Fargo slowly pushed the Colt back into the holster, his eyes taking in the tremendous size of the figure. The man stood six-four and weighed at least two-fifty, he guessed. Fargo's glance went to the heavy black-bearded face, lined, with cruel lips that turned down at the corners. He wore buckskin pants and a red shirt. Arms like small trees reached out from the rolled-up sleeves of his shirt. The man's eyes were black coals, cold and darting. "Who are you, mister?" his voice rumbled, and he stepped closer, splashing water with one foot as he did.

"Fargo," the Trailsman answered. "Skye Fargo. And you?"

"Manyon," the huge man said, and Fargo saw the brutish face behind the thick black beard as the man halted before him. "Never seen you up here before," the man rumbled.

"Never saw you, either," Fargo said calmly.

"You're working my trap lines," the huge figure blurted out.

Fargo frowned. "I put these trap lines down myself," he returned.

"I work this territory," the man accused.

"Where've you been till now?" Fargo thrust. "The summer's three-quarter gone."

"Taking care of the rest of my lines. This whole part of the mountain's mine," the man glowered.

"Shit it is. Nobody's got claim to this land and you know it," Fargo flung back.

"I'm making my own claim. Get your traps outa here and clear out. Besides, you're no mountain man. I know all the mountain men this side of the Tetons and you ain't one of them."

"I'm new around here, that's all," Fargo said.

"That ain't all," the huge man rumbled.

Fargo's eyes narrowed. "What the hell does that mean?" he shot back.

"I been lookin' at your traps. They ain't set down deep the way real mountain men do," the giant snapped. "And they're all new, every damn one of them new. Never seen no mountain man with all new traps in my life."

Fargo cast around quickly inside himself for the right words. This giant was a mountain man, but not the usual one. Too many questions. Mountain men didn't question, pry. They used words only to speak their mind. The rest was acting on it. This one had been sent to poke around. "Lost all my old traps in a mudslide. Had to get everything new," he said.

The giant flung out a hard sound, derisive. "A mountain man'd buy used traps afore he'd buy new ones, leastways half of them. Takes a year to get the new smell out of a trap," the man said.

Fargo cursed silently. The big brute knew his trapping. "I figured to do the best I could," Fargo said.

"Shit you did. You're an outsider nosin' around for

somethin' up here. Now you get out of here. Take your gear and keep going," the man rasped.

Fargo's mouth drew tight. No good would come from backing off. "Go to hell," he said softly. "I can trap any damn place I want."

The giant stared at him for a moment, his heavy brutish face glowering. His response took the Trailsman by surprise two ways. First, he didn't think the man would go for someone with a gun in a holster. Second, he didn't expect the quickness of the huge figure. The man hurtled himself forward in an arching dive, springing from the balls of his feet without a second's warning. Fargo started to crouch, half-turn as he saw the huge form hurtle toward him. He'd just gotten the Colt half out of the holster when the giant slammed into him like a grizzly bear. Fargo felt himself going down, twisting, falling on his shoulder. The ground came up to hit him with a jarring shock, and the heavy figure pressed down over him from above. He managed to get the Colt out only to feel it smashed from his hand by a thunderous blow that made his wrist tremble.

But the giant had to lean to the side to knock the Colt loose. Fargo twisted savagely as the weight lifted for an instant. He rolled from under the giant, kept rolling, felt one huge arm miss him by an inch as it thundered into the ground. Fargo whirled and regained his feet in one quick motion, in time to see Manyon rising, starting to set himself for another charge. Fargo swung, felt his blow land on the heavy beard, which acted like a cushion. Yet it was hard enough to snap the giant's head back. Fargo followed it with a roundhouse left that landed on the man's cheekbone, sending him falling back on one knee. He brought a looping right up from his boots, saw it knock the giant backward to the ground.

The man loosed a roar that shook the trees. He rolled as Fargo aimed a kick at him that missed, came up on his feet. Fargo glanced around, spied the Colt lying a dozen feet away, and made the mistake of trying to reach it. He was only halfway to it when he had to spin around as he heard the thundering figure bearing down on him. He drove a straight right at the brute face, using all his shoulder behind it. With a quickness that surprised once again, the man slipped his head to one side and Fargo felt the blow only graze the side of the jaw. He tried to duck away from huge arms that flung themselves around him, but the man refused to be stopped and the Trailsman felt himself seized, lifted, flung like a rag doll. He slammed into a thick tree trunk, gasped in pain, and had time only to partly avoid a thunderous blow that caught him high atop the head. He flipped halfway around the base of the tree, flashing purple and yellow dots filling his eyes. Grass and dirt pressed into his palms and he knew he was on the ground.

He was shaking his head when the giant arm caught him from behind, went around his neck, lifted. Fargo's breath vanished at once and he was lifted, flung again into the tree, this time hitting into it on his side. He dismissed the thought of fighting back until he could clear the haze from his eyes and he rolled along the ground as though he were a rug being unrolled, felt the air rush past him as the man aimed a kick that barely missed landing. Fargo crashed into a clump of brush, shook his head, and half-fell, half-stumbled through the brush, felt more than saw the huge form just behind him. He heard the man roar again, lunge for him, and he spun, dived sideways, and heard the heavy figure crash into the brush, roar out curses.

Fargo shook his head and the haze lifted. The big man was just regaining his feet, rising up from the brush like some half-human apparition coming to life. Fargo backed away as the man came at him again, lips drawn back in a grimace of a grin. The giant lunged, swung hammer fists, but Fargo parried both blows, ducked under a third. He tried a hard left that landed against the end of the thick black beard. The giant shook it off as though it had been a mosquito sting, swung again with his tree-trunk arms. Fargo ducked, stayed low, avoided a succession of blows as he gave ground. His extra hunting knife was still in the sheath strapped to his calf, but the huge figure wasn't giving him the moment he needed to reach down and pull it out. The stream was behind him, only a few feet back, and he moved toward it. He reached down, tried to get his fingers to the knife, but the figure dived forward with another roar of curses. Fargo twisted away, barely managed to avoid the clutching hands. He brought a sweeping blow around in a wide arc, sank it deep into the giant's midsection, and was rewarded with the huge gasp of breath that rushed from his opponent.

The man halted, staggered back for a step, and Fargo brought up a short uppercut, putting his back behind the blow. It caught the giant flush on the point of the chin, and this time Fargo felt his fist go past the cushion of the beard. Manyon went backward, fell, landing on his heavy rear, astonishment on his face. Fargo stepped forward, came in close, and aimed a kick at the man's jaw. The giant snapped his head to the side, again so surprisingly quick for his size, the kick only grazing his face. He brought one huge arm up, wrapped it around Fargo's leg, and pulled; the Trailsman fell forward, hitting the ground almost in front of the giant. He tried to roll away, but the treelike arms came down on him, a blow into the middle of his back that felt as though a mule had kicked him.

Fargo gasped out in pain, managed to twist to the side, and took the second blow on his shoulder. He got to his feet as the huge form came hurtling at him again, tried a right cross that met only flailing arms, felt himself sent reeling backward. Hitting the ground, he took another kick as he rolled away, absorbing only half the force of it, but he felt his strength fading, his back burning with pain. He rose, avoided two more crushing blows, stuck a sharp jab into the giant's face, and darted away from another blow. The man's eyes burned with fury as he pressed forward. Fargo backed toward the stream again, moving toward the place where he'd reset the underwater beaver trap. The huge figure came toward him relentlessly. He flicked two more jabs out as he kept backing, the blows disregarded entirely by the giant. Fargo parried another two sledgehammer blows, felt the force of them jar his arms, kept moving backward. He was almost at the stream, glanced quickly over one shoulder to make certain of the spot.

He took another step back, his right foot at the edge of the stream now. Suddenly he let himself seem to slip, his foot slide out behind him, and he dropped to one knee. With a roar of glee, the giant rushed at him. Fargo held his position, counting off split seconds. As the man's body reached him, he dived down, felt the blows go over his head. He came up, both shoulders catching the man just under the knees. He was thrown backward by the force and weight of the hurtling form, but he saw the giant fly over him in an arc to come down in the middle of the stream.

The sound of the trap snapping shut was all but muffled, but the terrible scream resounded through the forest, rising up only for an instant to end in a guttural gargling sound. Fargo pulled himself around on one knee. The huge form lay facedown in the stream, the massive legs kicking in a final spasm and then stretching out in stiff stillness. Fargo circled to the left, stepped into the stream where the water was already turning red. The man's head had hit the trap. Steel teeth had all but severed his jaw from his neck. Fargo straightened up, looked away for a moment, drew in deep breaths, and felt the burning ache of his every muscle. He returned his eyes to the grisly scene, moved around the top of the man's head, and freed the chain where the trap was anchored to a stone. He reached down, got hold of an arm and dragged the figure, even heavier in death, pulled the body from the stream and into the woods. He rested a moment, then continued dragging the body deeper into the woods as the trap stayed fastened onto the giant's face like a gruesome steel mask. He dragged the figure until he found a low, small cave in a rocky area, pushed the body into it as far as it would go.

He left it there, paused to regain his breath, and started back toward the stream. The giant had been sent to check his traps. He'd been no mountain man simply angered by the presence of a newcomer. He was a contact. The phony surveyors, perhaps. They could have circled back and told him to look into the new mountain man. Or he might have done so on his own. But not just out of curiosity. He'd been examining the traps in detail, searching for signs, wary of something. And he'd found what he sought. But it was an act no mountain man would ordinarily set out to do. The ugly brute had been more than the usual mountain man.

Fargo's eyes were hard as he retraced steps back to the stream. The giant had followed the stream for a good distance, perhaps days. The legs of his leather trousers had been wet up to the knees and the moccasins soaked through, Fargo recalled noticing. He'd walked in the stream to avoid leaving tracks, of course. But somewhere, he had a cabin. It could be worth finding and searching the place, Fargo pondered as he stepped over the stream. Tomorrow, he told himself quickly, after a night's rest for his battered body, which ached in every muscle. He picked up the pelts and slowly returned to his cabin.

Suni, taking skins down from the drying rack, saw his bruises at once and rushed to him, deep eyes wide with concern. He managed a grin of reassurance for her, and as she took the pelts, he went to his saddlebag and fetched the Gilead-bud salve he always carried. Inside the cabin he stripped, lay in front of the warmth of the fire, and let Suni rub his body with the salve. He fell asleep before she finished and the night descended.

4

When he woke in the morning, she was curled up beside him as usual, the blanket over both of them. He rose, stretched carefully, found his aches were gone for the most part. He had coffee brewed when she rose and he spoke to her as he sipped from the steaming mug.

"I have to go away. A day, maybe two or three, I don't know," he told her, using a mixture of English and Sioux.

"Suni take care of traps." She nodded.

"Good. You've plenty to eat in the house," he said, eyeing the slabs of venison now ready for cooking. She put her arms around his neck, pulled herself close to him.

"Fargo careful," she murmured. "Suni wait."

He hugged her and rose, and she helped him saddle the pinto. He'd decided to take the horse, uncertain what he might find in the fastness of the mountains. He waved to the girl as she watched from the doorway until he was out of sight of the cabin. He rode alongside the stream, making no effort to hurry. The ugly giant had covered his tracks with the stream, but he had to step onto the land from time to time, Fargo knew. He'd find the right places to read the banks of the swift-running water, he was certain.

The stream wandered its way through the mountains and Fargo saw a large flock of wild turkeys and was sorry he hadn't time to bring one down. He'd gone most of the day when the stream met with a second stream coming down from high in a mountain ridge. Fargo dismounted, carefully stepped to where the two streams joined, his eyes searching the ground. He halted, grunted in satisfaction as he found it, the imprint of a moccasin on the soft soil just above the spot where the streams joined.

He remounted, turned, and followed the second stream. The land rose steeply and bordered the edge of thick forest growths. Night dropped quickly over the mountains and Fargo made camp beside the stream. He dined on beef jerky and washed it down with the clear, cold mountain water, slept in his bedroll until the dawn returned to filter grayness through the forest at his back. He was in the saddle, climbing with the stream again by the time the sun made its way through the foliage.

The Wind River Mountains held many forbidding faces, he was beginning to realize as he rode through areas far wilder than where he had built his cabin. A stretched-out slope of bare-faced rock made a jagged scar in the distance and the stream continued to make its way across the side of the mountain, almost horizontally now. Suddenly he came upon a high mountain valley, a long narrow area bordered by tall pine-forested sides. He spotted the cabin through a break in the pine trees, headed for it, spurring the pinto into a trot. The cabin door hung open, he saw as he reached the log house. He dismounted, called out. Only silence answered. But the open door and the emptiness meant little. It might not be the cabin he sought, the owner merely off somewhere tending his trap lines. Fargo stepped forward, paused in the open doorway. The cabin was larger than the hasty one he had created, a small half-room in the back. His eyes scanned the interior of the main room and

61

his mouth tightened for a brief moment. It was the cabin he sought. Three wool shirts on a wall peg provided the answer, far too large to fit an ordinary man.

He stepped inside, his eyes sweeping the room, taking in a crudely built table, a large iron pot, a sack of stonemeal in one corner. Pelts were atop each other in the adjoining half-room, mostly possum, and he stepped into the area, saw more clothes tossed in a heap on the floor, leather pants and jackets and a heavy fur outercoat. He saw something else in a corner, a wood box closed with a crude pin latch.

He picked it up, carried it to the table in the other room, and pulled the peg free of the hand-made latch. He opened the box, stared down at a packet of square slips of paper. He ruffled through them. Each bore the word RECEIPT in heavy black lettering. Below, a blank space for a signature or initials was underlined by a single, straight line. Under the line he saw the words: *Rocky Mountain Fur Co.* He reached down to a larger sheet of paper folded together and wedged into the bottom of the box, pulled it out. He unfolded it and frowned as he read what was plainly a list written in hand, a scrawling but legible script.

> Jake Boomer—High Ground
> Albert Cajun—Two Peaks
> Mountain John—Sunrise Lake
> Canadian Pete—Piney Woods
> Sam Tall—Dogface Mountain
> Able Heller—Old Trail Camp
> Moose Mackinaw—Deep Wood
> Indian Solo—Ponca Hills
> Fortman—Back Hundred
> Tolliver—Timberline Ridge
> Easeman West—North Face
> Stonewood Sam—Teton Face

Fargo stared at the list for a few minutes, then folded it again, put it back at the bottom of the box. It was plainly a list of most of the mountain men and the Wind River areas where they did their trapping. The ugly brute had been some kind of on-the-spot contact man. He closed the box and put it back where he'd found it. The pieces were taking shape, the operation based on contacts, information, timing, and the illiterate independence of the mountain men. His thoughts broke off at once as he heard the sound of the horse outside. He turned to the door, the Colt in his hand instantly. The cabin was hardly the place for casual visitors. He was moving toward the door when he heard the call from outside, felt the frown dig into his brow. It was a woman's voice.

"Mister Manyon? You in there?" the voice called.

Fargo stepped into the doorway, saw the trim figure standing beside a big bay gelding, the short brown hair topping the pert face that broke open in astonishment, only a little more so than his own visage.

"*You!*" Sally Bowers exclaimed. Her eyes flicked to the pinto. "I thought that horse looked familiar," she snapped. "Where's Mister Manyon?"

Fargo let his shoulders shrug. "Not here," he said.

"But you're here, sneaking around again, snooping, same as you were doing at my brother's office," she flung at him, bright brown eyes flashing fire. "Is that all you ever do?"

"No," he said calmly. "I go after swindlers and cheats."

"You mean you repeat Caroline Stanton's lies," the girl said hotly.

Fargo studied her. The anger was no act, just as real as it had been that day at the warehouse. But she was here to see the ugly brute, and that said even more. Yet she didn't fit into the picture. Not yet, anyway.

"What's a girl like you doing up here alone? This is damn wild country," he said.

"My brother sent me to get something from Mister Manyon, not that it's any of your business," she returned.

"Your brother?" Fargo echoed, his brows lifting.

63

"Doesn't seem he cares much about you, sending you up here alone."

Her face grew stiff with fury. "How dare you? My brother knows very well that I can take very good care of myself," she flung at him.

Fargo grunted derisively. "Sure you can," he said. "How often have you been up in these mountains?"

"This is the first time," she said. "But that's no matter."

"Of course not," Fargo said, letting the sarcasm hide his racing thoughts. Craig Bowers held the reins, that was growing damn clear. But he also carefully kept in the background, even to callously sending his own sister to risk her neck and run interference for him. He was getting to dislike Craig Bowers without ever having met the man, Fargo decided. "Manyon sell to your brother?" he asked, keeping his tone casual.

"Yes," the girl said. "And you'd best get out of here before Mister Manyon comes back. I hear he's no man to get angry."

"You never met him, then," Fargo pressed.

"No," Sally Bowers said.

"I happen to know he won't be back soon," Fargo told her.

"I'll wait," she said haughtily.

"I'd say not for a few days, at least," Fargo pushed.

"Then I'll just bed down here until he returns. I've supplies to wait for a week if I must," she said. He saw her eyes turn suspicious as she looked at him. "How do you know he won't be back soon?" she asked.

"Somebody told me," he answered.

The suspicions stayed in her eyes. "I don't think I believe anything you say," she decided aloud. "I'll just stay and wait."

"Suit yourself." Fargo shrugged, stepped to the pinto, and pulled himself onto the horse. She wore a dark-green shirt and her breasts were as he remem-

64

bered, as saucy and pert as the rest of her, pressing the shirt out with sharp, upturned points. Her sassy face seemed even more so as she turned it up to him with anger.

"Don't come nosing around while I'm here. You'll get yourself shot," she warned.

His glance went to the .38 on her hip, and he grinned down at her. "I'll remember that," he said, saw her eyes flash. He turned the pinto and rode slowly away, to disappear into the heavy tree cover. The grin had left his face almost at once. Sally Bowers had become an unexpected problem. She'd soon conclude that something had happened to the ugly giant when he failed to show up at the cabin. He couldn't let her go back to tell Craig Bowers that. The man would be quick to grow alarmed. He'd grow extra careful and see that his agents made no new contacts. They'd make him no offer for his pelts and pay with a phony receipt. Without that, the entire plan was a failure, the summer's masquerade a waste, and Craig Bowers still very much in business. Everything hung on Bowers including him in his operation. Dammit, there was only a little time to go before they'd start making their buying contacts, Fargo muttered angrily. He had to find a way to send Sally Bowers back without arousing suspicions.

He rode with his lips tightened in grimness, halted after a half-dozen miles as he saw dusk begin to settle, the problem still unsolved. He'd sleep on it, he decided, found a hollow, and made a small fire for himself as night cloaked the mountains. The dilemma danced in the flames mockingly as he discarded one idea after another. When he finally pulled the blanket from his bedroll over himself, he had formed part of a decision. He'd return to her, concoct a story about the ugly brute that would let her go back without suspicions. It would buy time, and time was important now. He needed only enough to let Craig Bowers send his agents out to do their buying. Bowers would stay in the background, he felt certain. He could see how the man made his moves, taking care. He probably went out of his way to let Caroline Stanton see that he was in town. Fargo grunted, turned on his side. He had a piece of convincing to do in the morning. Maybe it wouldn't be all that difficult. Maybe the night alone in the Wind River Mountains would make her happy to hightail it back home. The stark loneliness had a way of shriveling the spirit unless you were used to it. He slept, hoping the mountains would give him some help.

He woke with the sun, washed, used the mountain stream, and then retraced his steps back to the narrow mountain valley where the cabin stood. She was outside when he reached it, just buttoning on a yellow blouse, stuffing the tails into her skirt. She looked up as she heard him, and he saw her hand dart out to a stump nearby, yank the gun from the holster lying atop it. She lowered the gun as he came into view, riding slowly toward her. She watched him halt and swing down to the ground, start toward her.

"That's far enough," she said, raising the gun partway. "I told you not to come nosing around here again."

"Didn't come for that," Fargo said. "Came to tell you something."

"Such as?" she asked, lowering the gun a fraction.

"About Manyon," he said blandly. "He won't be back for a spell. Went and hurt himself. Had to hunt up a doctor."

Her eyes held skepticism. "Where'd you hear that?"

"Mountain man I met yesterday," Fargo said casually.

"What happened to Mister Manyon?" she asked, bright brown eyes sharp.

"Slipped on a wet rock with an arm full of pelts. Cracked a leg bone, it seems, more than he could doctor himself," Fargo said. "No sense in your waiting for him. You might as well go back yourself. Can't tell when he'll come back."

He saw her lips purse as her eyes stayed on him. "I see," she murmured. "You'd like that, wouldn't you?"

He frowned at her. "How's that?"

"You'd like me to go back. The place would be all yours to snoop around in some more," she said.

"I did all the snooping I needed to do," he shot back. "I just thought you'd like to know you'd no need to expect him soon."

He saw her eyes soften for an instant. "All right then, thank you for coming to tell me," she said, and he began to smile. "But I'm still staying."

His smile vanished. "What the hell for?" he blurted.

She half-shrugged. "My brother's gone to Casper. He won't be back till the end of the month. It's beautiful here and I'm sure Mister Manyon will appreciate my watching his cabin for him. I'll just wait. I've no hurry to get back to town."

Fargo felt his lips tighten. Damn, she'd bought the story and it still turned out wrong. "This is no country for a slip of a girl alone, dammit," he barked.

He saw her eyes turn haughty. "I told you once before, I can take very good care of myself," she said. "You just can't believe that, can you?"

"You've got it right there," he snapped back.

"No, of course you couldn't buy that. Your type thinks a woman is just helpless without a big handsome man like you around," she said.

"Thanks. Glad you noticed," Fargo interrupted.

Her eyes narrowed a fraction. "I noticed. You're big and good-looking in an insufferable, conceited way. You're also very wrong. You don't know me," she said.

"I know these mountains and I know the ugly varmints, two-legged and four, you can find here," he said. "It's no damn place for you to stay alone."

"I told you, I can take care of myself," she said crisply. She reached out, took the gun belt from the stump, and strapped it on, shoved the gun in the hol-

67

ster. She turned to face him squarely, paused, snapped her hand to the holster, and drew. She was fast, faster than most men, he saw in silence.

"Let's see you do better," she said smugly as she returned the gun to the holster. Fargo's hand moved, quick as a snake's strike, and the Colt seemed to leap into his hand, all in one split-second motion. He saw her eyes widen as she stared into the gun barrel. "Very impressive," she said quietly. She drew her gun, turned to where a row of big brown-centered sunflowers lined one edge of the trees. She fired two shots and two sunflowers disappeared. Fargo's shots came so fast they sounded as one, and the next two sunflowers vanished. Her eyes went back to him, new respect in them again. "All right, you're very good, but you must admit I'm hardly an amateur," she said. "You're too egotistical to say it," she added smugly.

She'd been damn good, but he wasn't about to tell her so and his experienced eye had seen something more. "Target-range shooting. College-girl shooting. Not enough out here," he rasped.

"Dammit, you just can't admit I can take care of myself," she returned hotly.

"Not enough, I told you. Could you put two holes in a man?" he flung at her. He caught the moment of hesitation. "You just answered," he said coldly.

"I just never thought about it, that's all. I could if I had to," she said.

"You won't have time to think up here. Shooting's only part of it," he said. He bored down, trying to shake her, scare her into going back. "Ever meet with a hungry cougar? You know how to tell if a grizzly's out to warn or to kill?" he threw at her.

"I'll learn. Everyone has to learn," she said.

He grunted derisively. "You learn with somebody who can teach you. You don't learn to swim by jumping into the middle of a lake. And there's many that never make it. It takes having what I call a wild sense. Like now, you don't feel that diamondback behind you."

Her eyes widened and she whirled, yanking the gun out. Fargo's hand shot out like the snake that wasn't there, closed around her wrist while his other hand pushed up on her elbow. He twisted and her arm bent forward. "Ow!" she gasped as the gun fell to the ground. He spun her around, sent her stumbling backward with a shove.

"Sure you can take care of yourself," he said grimly. "Go home, honey, while you can."

"Bastard," she said, glaring, rubbing her arm. "You tricked me. That wasn't fair."

"Fair?" he half-shouted back. "Fair's only a word up here. There's nothing fair up here and every damn thing can trick you. There's only surviving and not surviving, and most times you don't get to take back your mistakes."

She studied him for a long moment. He'd reached her, he told himself. Dammit, he'd reached her finally, saw it in her eyes, and then she clipped out words through tight lips. "I'll stay awhile. Maybe he'll come back soon," she said.

He spun around, holding back his anger, and climbed onto the pinto. "You're a stubborn little fool," he bit out.

"Let's say I've more confidence in myself than you have," she said.

He kept his face stern, tried one more time. "Confidence is one thing. Stupid's another," he growled.

Her eyes flashed and she tilted her chin up. "You can go now," she said. He heard her call out as he spun the pinto around. "Have you found a name for yourself yet?" she asked.

"Fargo," he called back. "Skye Fargo." He slapped the horse on the rump and galloped away, not looking back, slowing only when he was into the thickness of the forest. "Goddamn," he spit out. Stubborn little package. He hadn't lied to her about survival in these mountains, only laid it on thick. And he'd reached her, but she had too much arrogance in her to back down. His lips bit down on each other. He had to get

69

her to leave before she had time to suspect the truth, that the big ugly brute wasn't coming back ever. Damn, he had to find a way.

The sound of a waterfall caught his ears and he followed it, climbed onto a ridge where a small waterfall cascaded down a wall of exposed rock. He dismounted as the pinto drank, then cooled himself under the gently tumbling water. Leaning against the rocks, Fargo racked his brain to find another way to send Sally Bowers back to town without a head full of suspicions. Answers proved hard to find, however. She'd bought his story about Manyon having hurt himself, but he couldn't come up with a way to carry that any further. He found himself hoping she might just decide on her own to go back after a few days. It was a possibility he couldn't afford to depend on. She had too much sass and spunk to fold up quickly, damn her!

Swearing softly, he stretched, stepped onto a rock, and found himself looking over a fold in the terrain, the narrow valley half-hidden below. The strand of smoke in the distance caught his eye, on the other side of the little valley and the cabin. He watched it for a moment. "Campfire," he murmured to himself, fanning out too low to the ground to be a chimney. He felt the frown push across his forehead. The smoke was beyond the valley and the cabin a bit too close for another mountain man. His eyes narrowed as he peered across the distance. He stepped from the rock, pulled the pinto from beneath the watery spray of the falls, rubbed the saddle dry, and mounted. He climbed in a long half-circle, skirting the valley's narrow stretch, working his way toward the smoke. When he'd come to a line with it, he began to move down, walking the horse slowly.

He dismounted as he came close enough to smell the fire. Deer meat being roasted. He tethered the pinto on a low branch and moved through the trees, silent as a wraith, halted as the little clearing came into view. Three men squatting around the fire, chewing greedily on the meat. His eyes scanned the trio. Seedy, tattered outfits. They ate nervously, tearing off bites, the way men who'd been on the run eat. The nearest one had a rodentlike face with little eyes, and the one beside him seemed all bones, his skin drawn tight over his face. The third one ate with uneven yellowed teeth in a face that was filled with cruelty.

On the run from something, Fargo reckoned. He'd seen too many like them over the years. They'd chosen to flee over the mountains and only desperate men would choose that route. Desperate, ruthless men who'd stop at nothing. Fargo straightened, peered down through the trees behind him to where the narrow valley stretched out, barely visible from where he had halted. But the trio would surely cut through the valley. It was the logical and the best path to take. They'd come on to the cabin and Sally Bowers, set on her like hawks on a baby rabbit.

Fargo dropped low, began to move backward as the three men finished their meal and began to put out the fire. He reached the pinto and climbed into the saddle. His problem was solved. When the trio finished with Sally Bowers, she'd not be wondering about the missing mountain man. There'd be no more waiting for him. She'd be grateful to drag herself back to Wind River. When Craig Bowers finally returned, there'd be no talk about the ugly giant, only what had happened to her. Fargo rode slowly back the way he had come, circling the edge of the little valley, rode past the tip of it, and started the long journey toward his own cabin. Three pack rats would buy him the month he needed and Craig Bowers would have to set his operation in motion without word from his contact man. The problem was solved.

"Like hell," Fargo bit out aloud as the pinto nosed down the slope. The goddamn problem wasn't solved at all. It had been compounded. He reined the pinto to a halt and swore again. He couldn't go off and

71

leave the girl to those stinking cutthroats. They might just as likely kill her when they finished with her, he knew. Damn, just as like as not. If he saved her hide, he'd have the whole damn problem back in his lap again. He wheeled the pinto around. "No choice," he muttered angrily to himself, "no goddamn choice." He started back toward the narrow little valley, cussing pretty little females with more spunk than sense, more arrogance than ability.

He felt his jaw tighten as he made his way back. The trio had probably spotted the cabin by now, he guessed. But they'd hang back. No careless moves, not those three. Stray dogs used to being chased learn to be careful. He led the pinto into a thicket of heavy pine, swung to the ground, and went the rest of the way on foot until he reached a spot with a clear view of the cabin. Sally was outside, wringing out a shirt, wearing a skirt and the top of her slip. She had nice shoulders, square, well-formed, and the saucy breasts pushed out even more pertly under the thin cotton of the slip. He settled down and waited. It wasn't a long wait. The girl went into the cabin with the wrung-out shirt, reappeared buttoning a cotton checked blouse over the upturned breasts. She saw the lone horseman appear, moving slowly out from the line of trees at the side of the cabin. Fargo saw her hand go to the gun at her hip at once.

He moved forward a little more, inching his way. The rider was the one with the rodentlike face. The man dismounted, started toward Sally Bowers. "Well, now, what's a little lady like you doin' out here alone?" he said with a mockery of a grin. "Seems to me you need company," he added.

Fargo saw Sally draw her gun, her eyes flash instant fire. "Get back on that horse, mister. Fast," she barked.

The man halted. "Now, that's not friendly," he said.

"I'm not friendly," Sally answered, drew the ham-

72

mer back on the gun. "I'll shoot, mister," she said. The man took a step backward, turned his palms up.

"I believe you would, little lady," he said, took another step backward, dropped to one knee. "All I want is some food," he almost whined. Fargo watched Sally, saw the hesitation pass over her face. "Anything you can spare," the man wheedled. Fargo watched Sally's eyes, uncertainty in them as she concentrated on the figure in front of her. She was completely unaware of the two other figures coming up behind the cabin on foot, running bent over out of the trees. They came up on both sides of the cabin, halted at each corner.

"Drop the gun, honey," the one called. Sally whirled, eyes leaping from one to the other, saw the two guns trained on her. Fargo watched as she swallowed hard, still holding the gun but aware the odds were against her. "Drop it, girlie," the one with the yellowed teeth repeated. She never had a chance to obey, for the first one came up behind her, threw one arm around her neck, and grabbed hold of the gun with his other hand. The other two were there in an instant, pulling the gun from her helpless fingers and smashing her across the face with a backhanded blow. Fargo heard her sharp cry of pain.

He saw her kick out, catching the tight-skinned, bony one in the crotch with the kick. He gasped out pain as he fell to his knees. "Oh, Christ. Kill the bitch," the man screamed.

The rodent-faced one answered by seizing Sally's skirt, pulling it up almost over her head, and bringing his knee up hard into her buttocks to send her sprawling forward. "No, no, Harry. We got some funnin' to do with her first. Come on, you ain't killed. You'll get your turn," the man said.

"I'm going to split her ass, that's what," the other one said, pulling himself to his feet. The other two yanked the girl to her feet, started to drag her into the cabin, and the thin-faced one followed, still holding himself.

Fargo let his breath out in a slow sigh, pulled the big Colt from his holster, and got to his feet. He moved to one side of the cabin, left the cover of the trees in a long loping crouch. From inside the cabin he heard Sally scream, then the sharp sound of a slap, another gasp of pain, and then her voice rising. "No, owoooooo . . . no, damn you, no!" He heard her cry out again in pain. He moved alongside the cabin to the open door. There was no anger in his strong face, only the annoyance of a man having to do a faintly irritating task. Reaching the door, he moved on silent feet, swung himself into the doorway. Sally was almost standing on her head. Two of the men had her upside down, her legs spread out. The third one was starting to rip her petticoat away.

"Hurry up, Zeke," the one called. "Let's get us a piece of that beaver."

Fargo crouched, took aim with the Colt. He was about to shoot when Sally twisted her torso and the rodent-faced one lost his grip on one leg. She fell on her side, kicking, and the other man brought a blow down into her ribs. Fargo heard the cry of pain escape her and then the two attackers half-rolled, half-flipped her onto her back. The rodent-faced one fell atop her, pushing her petticoat up as he did so while the other one yanked her head back against the floor by seizing a handful of hair. The third one stopped holding his crotch and began tearing at her blouse, dropping to both knees.

"Give it to her good, Harry," he chortled.

Fargo, his face wrinkling in disgust, drew another bead on the trio, moving to his left as Sally Bowers screamed, and he saw the rodent-faced man pushing her legs apart roughly by ramming his fist between her thighs. Fargo waited a moment more, aimed carefully. His first shot hit the man atop the girl, slamming into the side of his face. The man toppled to one side as though kicked by a mule, the nearest part of his face vanishing. The one holding her by the hair looked up, his jaw dropping open. Fargo's second shot went into his mouth and out the back of his head, and he catapulted backward to smash against the wall, slide to the ground, spilling red like a shattered wineglass. The third attacker managed to get his gun out, half-rose, when the Trailsman's shot blew his midsection almost in two. He collapsed forward as though he were a rag doll with the straw stuffing knocked out of it. Fargo saw Sally Bowers roll over, barely avoid the form that pitched forward. She stumbled to her feet, grasped Fargo's outstretched hand, and pulled herself to him, falling against his chest.

"Oh, God. Oh, my God," she breathed, and he held her shaking body with his left hand as he slipped the Colt back into its holster. She trembled against him and he felt her fight deep breaths into her lungs, stiffen her body until the quivering stopped. Finally she stepped back a pace, let her hands flutter at the torn blouse where glimpses of her breasts came through the shredded places. Her eyes lifted, sought his. Fargo kept his face stern, his eyes the blue of a cold November lake.

"They'd have killed me," she murmured.

"Probably," he said. "Afterward."

He saw the shudder run through her as she stared into space for a moment, returned her gaze to him. "Who were they?" she questioned.

"Drifters. Running from the law. I'd bank on that," Fargo said.

She shuddered again, turned from him, and stepped out of the cabin. He followed and watched her draw breath in deeply, then turn back to him. "If you hadn't come back . . ." she said, let the sentence trail off, horror in her eyes. "I owe you," she said. "I'm alive because of you."

Fargo made no reply and saw the little frown appear on her brow as she gazed at him.

"How did you manage to come back at the right moment?" she asked.

He half-shrugged. "Just happened by."

Her frown stayed, deepened a fraction as her eyes stayed on him. "No, you left going off in the other direction," she said slowly. "You couldn't have just happened by. You had to come back."

Fargo kept his face expressionless. "I saw the smoke from their campfire and went to have a look," he answered.

The frown grew still deeper. "Then you knew they'd come this way," she said.

"More or less," he said blandly.

Her face took on gathering anger. "You could have come by and warned me," she said.

"No need," he said with calm innocence. "You can take care of yourself. You told me so, remember?"

He watched her mouth tighten and fire leap into her eyes. She was glaring at him now. "Then you watched. You saw the whole thing. You could've stepped in any time," she spit out.

"I wanted to see you take care of yourself," he said affably.

She continued to glare at him, her lips drawn tight. "I almost liked you," she said finally.

"Sorry about that," he remarked.

"I can still take care of myself," she snapped. "Anybody can make one mistake."

"I told you, one mistake is all you get up here," he said. "Get your things together."

"Nonsense. I'll be all right now. I'm staying. Maybe Mister Manyon will be back sooner than you think," she said.

He looked at her through narrowed eyes, let his breath out in a long sigh. "He won't be back at all," Fargo said coldly.

"What's that mean?" She frowned.

"It means the ugly bastard is dead," Fargo said.

"How do you know that?" she returned.

"Because I made him dead," Fargo snapped, saw the shock flood her face. "It was that or letting him kill me and I didn't favor that much. That's what he came to do, though."

76

She backed, let herself sit down on the tree stump. Still frowning, her eyes wide, she looked up at the Trailsman. "Why'd he want to do that? Kill you?" she asked.

"He'd decided I wasn't a real mountain man and figured it'd be best if I was out of the way," Fargo told her.

"Best?" she asked. "Best for who?"

"For your brother," Fargo said coldly.

She jumped to her feet, her eyes flashing fire at once. "You've no cause to say anything like that," she threw at him.

"Haven't I?" he growled.

"No," she barked.

"Your brother sent you up here to see him, didn't he?" Fargo asked. "He was a contact for your brother, right?"

"He sold to my brother. That doesn't mean what you're saying," she returned hotly.

He threw a hard glance at her, strode into the cabin, stepped over one of the dead bodies, and picked up the little wooden box he'd found. Bringing it outside, he opened it, took the receipts out, and pushed them at her. "Look at them hard, honey." he said. "Each one's stamped with the name of the Rocky Mountain Fur Company."

Sally Bowers stared at the sheaf of receipts, shuffled them through her fingers. "Now what's your brother's man doing with a box full of unsigned receipts from the Rocky Mountain outfit?" Fargo pressed.

She glanced at him, her eyes now full of uncertainty, the fury wiped away. "I . . . I don't know," she said weakly.

"I do," he snapped. "They're the receipts your brother's men take with them when they spread out and intercept the men on their way down from the mountains with their furs. Those are some of the phony receipts they sign and hand the trappers, not that many of them can read."

"There's some other explanation," she said, trying

to fight assurance back into her voice. "Craig wouldn't be involved in anything like this. There just has to be some other explanation."

"I'll damn well find out if there is, come fur-buying time. That's not far off now," Fargo said.

Her eyes studied him for a moment. "I see now," she said, thinking aloud. "You've set yourself up as a mountain man so whoever's doing this will come to you, too."

"Go to the head of the class," Fargo answered.

"It's not Craig," she said, lifting her chin, pulling arrogance around herself protectively.

"Maybe not, but I can't risk you going back to town to blow it all apart," Fargo said. "Until I find out, you'll be my guest up here."

"Your guest? Where?" she asked.

"At the little cabin I built," he said.

"You mean your prisoner," she said.

He shrugged. "Pick any word that suits you, but you're not going back till this is over one way or the other. Now get your things."

"You can't hold me prisoner. I'll run away," she threatened.

His laugh was harsh. "On foot in these mountains? Try it and you won't be around to learn the truth about anything," he said, paused. "Or maybe you're afraid of the truth," he added.

She lifted her chin, glared back. "I'll say it again. I almost liked you for a minute." She brushed past him and went into the cabin. He went with her, saw her stop, swallow hard, step around the lifeless, bloody figures to scoop up her things. She was pale when she hurried outside past him. She drew a deep breath, turned to search his face.

"Reminders?" he said calmly.

She nodded. "Yes. You didn't have to come back. You could've let them take care of me and I'd be out of your hair."

"I slip up once in a while," he said.

"No, no slipup," she answered, studying his face.

"You're a strange man. You bend in an unbending way. And I owe you. I won't forget that. Somehow, I'll find a way to repay you."

"One of us will," he agreed, let his eyes go down to the saucy upturned breasts that pushed through the torn blouse. He saw her cheeks take on tiny dots of red, and she turned away, strode to where the bay gelding stood tethered. He walked to the pinto, swung into the saddle, waited for her to secure her things and mount. She swung in beside him as he started into the heavy forest terrain.

She rode silently beside him as he threaded the long way back across the ranges that made up the Wind River Mountains. They had crossed into the lower range when she spoke, tossing the question at him in midair. "What if I promise to say nothing to Craig if you let me go?"

"No sale," Fargo clipped out, not looking at her.

"Why not?" she asked.

"Blood's thicker than water," he said.

"Not always."

"Most of the time. Can't risk it."

"Don't you ever trust anybody?" she asked, exasperation in her voice.

"Sometimes," he said, ignoring her glare.

"What are you going to do when you find out you're wrong? What are you going to do about having held me prisoner for weeks?" she thrust.

He turned to her. "What if I'm right? What'll you do then?"

Her pretty face clouded at once, but she summoned up angry protectiveness. "I won't have to do anything. You're not right. I don't even have to think about that," she returned.

"You trying to convince me or yourself?" he slid at her.

She threw a glare of fury at him, spurred her horse on ahead, only slowed when the terrain grew thick. He came up alongside her unhurriedly, felt her glances, piercing, each a quick probe. She was silent again and then tried a new tack, her voice growing softer, full of reasonableness.

"You're too handsome a man to be so thick-headed," she said.

"You're too pretty to be so bland," he answered. Her lips tightened at once and he tossed her a grin. "Stop trying, honey. I don't take that kind of bait," he said.

Her eyes studied him, tiny lights in the depths of their brown orbs. "I guess not," she said. "My mistake. You're used to being flattered, I'm sure."

He turned from her. "Hold on, doll. It's steep from here on down," he warned, sent the pinto carefully over the top of the slope. He heard her gelding scramble for footing as the path led down the steep scrub brush. He let the pinto take his own way, half-turned in the saddle to see Sally Bowers half out of the saddle, trying to rein the gelding back as the horse slipped, stumbled, barely managed to stay on its feet. "Ease up, dammit," he yelled back at her. "Let your horse alone." He saw her slack the reins, grab hold of the saddle horn, and the gelding found footing on its own, picked its way slowly. Fargo returned to negotiating the rest of the steep slope, was waiting at the bottom when Sally arrived, and he saw the tiny beads of perspiration on her face. "Want to rest?" he asked.

She shook her head, drew a deep breath, and he watched the saucy breasts push out sharply against the torn blouse. Stubborn, prideful little character, he thought, rode on slowly, and gave her time to pull herself together. The remainder of the path moved sideways over the next range and the day had little left in it when Fargo spied the little cabin. Sally was a dozen yards back when he rode across the stream and into the little clearing of the cabin, swung down from the saddle. Suni ran from the cabin wearing only the deerskin skirt and the vest that covered almost nothing. She threw her arms around him.

"Fargo back. Suni happy," she said, hugging him.

He grinned down at the coppery beauty of her as she rested her head against his shoulder. Suddenly he saw the liquid eyes turn darker, a subtle change slip across the angular beauty of her face, and he knew Sally had come into the clearing. Suni's arms dropped from around him as her eyes fastened on Sally. He turned to see Sally had ridden up close and watched her swing lightly down from the gelding. Her eyes traveled up and down the Indian girl's lithe figure, shifted to Fargo. They held something more than surprise.

"My, oh, my," she murmured. "You didn't tell me how completely you were playing your role. Indian wife and all. I'm impressed. Or is she more than part of the masquerade?"

Her eyes waited with cool disdain and he ignored what he saw in them. "This is Suni," he said quietly. Sally's eyes roamed over the girl again as her head dipped in faint acknowledgment. Fargo saw an ominous stillness take hold of the Indian girl's face, her angular beauty suddenly made of ice. Suni's eyes stayed on Sally, unblinking. "Tie your horse and take your things inside," Fargo said, took the Indian girl by the arm, and led her around to the side of the cabin. He turned her to face him and saw the whirlpools of dark fury that were her eyes.

"Suni not good enough for Fargo. He bring new wife," she hissed.

He put his hand over her mouth. "No wife," he said. "But I have to keep her here. She must stay here."

"Why?" Suni glowered.

Fargo grimaced inwardly and knew the reasons were too complex, beyond explaining to her. He drew her against him, felt the soft warm breasts against his chest, cupped his hand around one. "Suni is Fargo's woman," he said.

She probed with her deep eyes. "But you bring her," she said.

He threw his hands up in a gesture of helplessness.

81

"I had to bring her," he repeated. "She must stay." He drew Suni to him again, held her, felt the stiffness in her body slowly relax. "It will be good. Like always," he said.

Her eyes found his, softening, but not completely. She accepted but reserved believing, followed him back to the front of the cabin. He stepped inside to see that Sally had put her things against one wall.

"Hardly a spacious hovel," she remarked with acid sweetness.

"You'll get used to it," he said. He took his shirt off, used the water bucket to wash, aware that Sally watched with approval, her eyes taking in the powerful shoulders, the broad, tight chest. He dried himself as Suni came inside, went to the simmering kettle on the fire, stirred it, and added another piece of venison. Fargo went to the half-dozen new pelts Suni had brought in during his absence, unrolled them to look at their condition. He tried to flatten them out, but they kept rolling up again and he saw Sally move to put her hand down at one end of the nearest pelt. She'd begun to reach for the skin when Suni was there, knocking her hand aside to clap her open hand on the pelt.

"No," the Indian girl hissed, her eyes pools of dark fury.

Sally Bowers pulled back, fright in her eyes for a moment; then, her jaw tightening, she started to answer.

"Shut up and sit down," Fargo growled.

Sally's glance flicked to him, anger in her eyes, then she let cool disdain take over.

"My, such sensitivity," she remarked tartly.

"Just sit down," he ordered quietly.

Sally turned away, went to the other side of the room, and sank down on the floor, allowing him a glance of tolerant amusement. The night descended and Suni left his side to stir the kettle again. Fargo put the flattened pelts atop the others.

"Food ready," Suni said. She took two trenchers

and two spoons, set them down for Fargo and herself. Fargo watched Sally rise, come over, the amused tolerance still in her eyes. She took another spoon and a trencher from the set he'd made and stacked in one corner. Suni dished the stew out to Fargo, then herself, commenced eating at once.

Sally's smile was cold as she dished her own food out. "Such jealousy," she said mockingly as she sat down cross-legged. "Tell her I'm hardly here to compete with her."

"She wouldn't believe me," Fargo said between mouthfuls.

"Why not?" Sally said, eyebrows lifting.

"She believes in the laws of nature. Simple, basic realities, the territorial threats, danger always near," he said.

"Primitive," Sally sneered.

"Real," he corrected. When the meal was over, Suni went outside, returned after a little while to spread the Indian blanket along the one wall. The fire had already burned to embers, the room darkening quickly. Fargo saw Sally rise, take her sleeping gear, and lay it out against the opposite wall. Suni stood upon the Indian blanket and he saw the deerskin skirt fall to the floor. With a wriggle of her shoulders she discarded the vest to stand in magnificent nakedness. Fargo rose, went to her, stepped out of his trousers, undressed to his shorts, and heard Sally's voice come across the almost-dark room, quiet shock in it.

"Aren't you going to hang a curtain or something?" she said.

"Wasn't figuring on it," Fargo said mildly.

"Well, figure on it, dammit," Sally's voice came back. "I haven't embraced your primitive life-style."

"Maybe you ought to try it," Fargo remarked pleasantly. It was too dark in the cabin for her to see the grin on his face, but she heard it in his voice.

"Damn you, Fargo. Act civilized. You're carrying this role too far," Sally hissed at him.

"Not acting at all, honey," he said, turning, and gathered an armful of the larger pelts. He took a length of lariat he had in the cabin, strung it across the center of the floor, suspended it from a peg on one wall and through a crack in a log on the other. He draped the pelts over the rope, paused to look down at Sally in the last of the firelight's glow. He could see only the dark silhouette of her form, but he felt her glare. "Sleep tight," he said, pulled his head back of the fur curtain.

He returned to lay down beside Suni's naked loveliness and felt her turn her back to him. Frowning, he pulled her around. "You want to please her," the Indian girl hissed.

"She is used to different ways," he explained.

Suni turned her back again. "You want to please her," she glowered into the wall. He took her shoulder, pulled her around again, slapped her cheek with two fingers, not hard, yet firmly enough to register his displeasure. Her form went limp at once and she twisted, her hands reached down to seize him, stroking him, her mouth tracing a path along his abdomen to encircle him, kissing, caressing with her tongue, making little sucking noises as her hands played along the inside of his thighs and abdomen. He felt the eagerness in her, the desperate wanting to please and be pleased, and he pulled her up, came into her at once. She thrust upward to meet him, the little cooing sounds accompanying each rhythmic thrust of her hips. He matched her quick, exploding passion, finding the deep copper breasts with his mouth. Dimly, he heard Sally leap to her feet, storm to the cabin door, the sound of her bedroll dragging behind her as she rushed outside. He did not stop, could not have had he wanted to, for he was exploding with Suni as she lifted her torso, powerful, lithe legs rising up to hold him in midair and the soft gasp drawn out, a voiceless cry.

Soon after, the girl lay curled up against him as she always did, asleep in moments. It wasn't long before

84

he heard Sally return to the warmth of the cabin, her bare feet padding hurriedly across the floor. He listened to her settle down near the embers in the fireplace on the other side of the fur curtain. She punched the pillow of her bedroll, the sound one of quiet fury. He smiled in the darkness and slept.

5

He woke to the smell of coffee brewing. Suni stood by the heavy enamel pot, brewing the liquid as he'd taught her to do. He pulled on trousers, washed at the bucket, and sipped the coffee the Indian girl handed him. He heard Sally stir on the other side of the pelts as he finished the coffee. He'd started to turn away when Suni began pulling the fur curtain down.

"No! Stop," he heard Sally cry out, but Suni continued to take down the furs; then he glimpsed Sally, dress held in front of her with one hand, grab the Indian girl's wrist as she was about to take down the last pelt. He saw Suni drop her hold on the pelt, her hands shoot out, go for Sally's throat. He was across the room in one leaping step, thrusting himself in front of Suni. Her deep eyes flashed fury at him as he pushed her back.

"No," he said softly but sharply. "*No!*" Suni looked at him through half-lowered lids for an instant, and his hand against her chest, he felt the steel-trap tension of her body. He pushed gently and the tension dropped away. "Get the traps," he said. "There's work to do."

She understood the statement inside the order, turned, and left the cabin on silent feet, a tiny shadow of satisfaction in her face. Fargo turned to Sally, saw she still held one of the trenchers in one hand, slowly lowered it. "I'll split her head if she comes at me again," Sally said angrily.

"You'll split nothing," Fargo told her. "It's over. Just don't provoke her, that's all."

"I didn't provoke her," Sally answered hotly.

"You grabbed her wrist. That's enough. You've got to understand someone like Suni. They react in different ways," he said.

He saw the cool disdain come into Sally's eyes as, brows lifted, she held his glance. "Such gallantry. The dashing knight in buckskin defending his lady's faults as well as her virtues," she intoned. "Only she's hardly a lady."

"She's a lot more woman than those you know. No exceptions, either," Fargo snapped back. He started for the door.

"How can you make love to that savage?" the girl shouted after him. "How can you?"

He paused. "Savagely," he tossed back, strode outside.

Suni was waiting with the traps and he knelt down beside her, began preparing the implements, spreading musk on one, asafetida on another, bear grease on a third. Sally came outside when he was finished, managing to look fresh and pert, he noted. Her glance at Suni passed over her with faint disdain that he knew the Indian girl picked up at once. Silently, he cursed Sally Bowers' pugnacious bitchiness. He walked past her, got the pinto, Suni's horse, and the gelding, and handed the reins to Suni.

"What are you doing?" Sally asked.

"Taking the horses with us to set the trap lines," he told her. "That way you won't get any fool ideas."

He tossed her a hunting knife. "Cut up the rest of the venison for tonight's supper," he said. "It's hanging high in a corner inside the cabin."

"I saw it," she said.

Fargo took the traps and started off, Suni following

with the horses tethered together. He went farther upstream than usual to set one of the traps, chose new territory for the other two. With Suni, he explored an area he hadn't used before, decided there was little point in trapping a new section with but a few weeks left to continue the charade. Suni found a little waterfall as they started to circle back, stripped off the deerskin dress, and bathed in the cool water as he watched the unsullied, unspoiled beauty of her. She dried herself with big box-elder leaves, curled up against him, and lay in his arms as the afternoon slid slowly away.

There was but an hour or so of day left when they returned to the cabin, and he saw something was wrong instantly: the cabin door tightly shut, the hunting knife on the ground. He dismounted, had just touched the ground when the door burst open and Sally ran out, her eyes wide.

"What happened?" he asked.

"A cougar. I just managed to get into the cabin," she said.

Fargo's eyes swept the little clearing. "Cougar's don't usually come prowling in broad daylight, not around a cabin," he said.

"The venison," she answered, and he frowned at her. "He smelled it and came for it," she said.

"How the hell long were you out here cutting it?" Fargo barked.

"I got tired. It was harder than I thought. I stretched out and napped awhile," Sally said.

"With the venison next to you," Fargo said, and she nodded. "You let it soften in the sun. No wonder he smelled it and came running."

"I woke and he was there, big yellow eyes. He snarled. I backed at first, then ran for the cabin and slammed the door behind me. He took the venison off with him."

"Shit," Fargo muttered.

"I'm sorry," she offered. "I didn't think anything

like that would happen. Can you shoot something else for supper?"

"Dusk light's the worst time for shooting, especially small game," Fargo answered, his brow furrowed. "No, we'll have us a green stew." He turned to Suni, spoke to her in Sioux, and she nodded. "Take her with you," he told the Indian girl. Her face stiffened, but she agreed with a flick of her eyes. He turned to Sally.

"Go with her," he ordered. "Keep your sassy mouth shut and do whatever she tells you to do." The girl's eyes narrowed, but she followed Suni into the forest. Fargo put the few pelts away, stabled the horses in the lean-to, and went into the cabin. It was dark when the two women returned, but he had the fire on and water simmering in the iron kettle. Sally staggered into the cabin, both arms full of roots, greenery, tubers, and flowers. She dropped it on the floor. Suni carried nothing at all and Sally glared at her first, then at Fargo. Her hands were brown with dirt and full of little scratches, he saw.

"She didn't do a thing except tell me what to pick or dig up," Sally protested.

"Who lost our supper?" Fargo threw back.

Her eyes lost their glare and she looked down at the greenery on the floor. "I think she had me picking a lot of stuff just for the hell of watching me," she grumbled.

"You're consistent, I'll say that for you," Fargo said, and she looked at him quickly. "You keep being wrong," he added, picking up the nearest batch of thin stems with bright-red clusters of pulpy food. "Strawberry spinach," he said. "The Indians use it all the time." He went on to the others she'd dropped to the floor. "Roseroot," he said of one set of four-inch stems. "Groundnut," he said of a chain of tuberlike bulbs on long roots. He hefted a cluster of long, wrinkled roots below a stack of white-petaled flowers. "Toothwort," he grunted. "Better than pepper in a stew." Suni was peeling the exterior skins from long

89

thin stalks topped with little magenta flowers, tossing the peeled stalks into the kettle. "Fireweed," Fargo said. "Heard enough?" he asked, and Sally nodded, looked silently at the floor.

Suni prepared the wild greens stew, the final result not only filling and tasty but nourishing, full of strong, fresh tastes. He waited till Sally finished her dish hungrily, leaned back. "Clever, aren't they, these savages," he remarked.

Her eyes met his coolly. "There's acquired knowledge and there's savagery. The one doesn't change the other. Keep that straight in your head," she said.

He grunted. Stubborn, arrogant little package, full of book learning. "There's smartness and there's wisdom. Keep that straight in your head," he said. She nodded back with a half-smile. Suni took the iron kettle outside to clean it out, and Fargo rose, unbuttoned his shirt, took it off, stretched his powerful deltoid muscles.

"You're not going to indulge yourself again tonight, are you?" Sally said, protest touching her voice.

"I sure hope so," Fargo said mildly.

Her eyes held haughty disdain. "Do you plan to exercise your animal drives *every* night?" she questioned stiffly.

"Why not?" he replied. "Can't see why it bothers you so much."

She drew iciness quickly around herself. "It doesn't bother me at all," she sniffed.

"Why'd you rush outside last night?" he asked.

"I felt like some fresh air," she said loftily.

He took her chin in one big hand. "Bullshit, sweetie." He smiled.

Her eyes flashed at once. "I'll stay right here tonight. I won't budge," she told him. "May I put up the curtain now?"

"Sure," he agreed, watched her take four pelts and drape them over the line. The room darkened quickly as the fire burned down and Suni returned, closed the cabin door to keep the warmth in the room. The darkness filled the cabin as Suni came to him on the Indian blanket, shed the deerskin dress, anxious to finish undressing him, to fondle and caress and revel in all her unspoiled, natural enjoyment of the senses. Less hurried than the night before, she derw out each soft cooing sound that was a part of her lovemaking, urged him on with the thrusting of her loins. His mouth on the coppery breasts pulled roughly, and she demanded more, moving her buttocks back and forth on the blanket, calling softly with little sounds. But there was another sound in the cabin, Sally's turning and tossing in her bedroll on the other side of the room. His smile in the dark was not just from the sheer pleasure of Suni's lovemaking. Then, as Suni's little gasps grew more urgent, he dimly became aware that the tossing and turning had stopped from behind the curtain. Later, Suni curled up beside him, he listened for sounds from across the cabin and heard none. He was only mildly surprised. Sally Bowers had the inner strength to discipline herself. He turned on his side and slept.

When the dawn came, he woke first, pulled on trousers, and peered behind the curtain of pelts. She was asleep, his wool hunting cap pulled down over her ears, the tip of her nose peeking out beneath it. Makeshift earmuffs, not self-discipline, he snorted silently. The quiet smile edged his lips again as he washed and dressed. Suni woke, went out to the brook, and returned, glistening, as he waited in the little clearing. Sally emerged in skirt and yellow blouse, managing to look pert.

"Sleep well?" he slid at her.

"Excellently," she tossed back. He went to fetch the Henry carbine, returned to address Suni.

"I'm going to get some meat for supper. You check the traps. Take the horses," he ordered, saw Sally maintain an expression of complete disinterest. He turned to her. "There's a splint broom in the corner.

91

Clean up the cabin. When you've done that, lay some feed in the lean-to."

He turned, not waiting for an answer, moving off in a different direction than the one he usually took to the trap lines. He slowed his pace and explored the cool green of the heavy forest. Deer stayed out of sight and even the hares proved elusive. He'd gone a good distance before he found an area with cottontails and snowshoes. He finally bagged two big snowshoe hares and started back to the cabin with them. It had taken considerably longer than he'd expected, and he walked briskly, saw the cabin come into sight through the trees. He saw something else and heard the single word drop from his lips. *"Shit!"*

Suni and Sally were outside the cabin, facing each other like two wildcats ready to pounce. Three pelts lay on the ground and he saw Suni point to them. Her voice echoed through the trees to him. "You clean," he heard her say.

"Do it yourself," Sally's answer shot back.

"You clean," Suni repeated, and Fargo heard the ominousness in her voice.

"I'm not your servant. Don't tell me what to do," he heard Sally shout back. He broke into a run as he saw Suni's hand shoot out, the blow catching Sally against the side of the face, knocking her down. Suni leaped on her at once, but he saw Sally twist, bring her fist backhanded to catch Suni across the shoulders. Suni missed her objective and Sally grabbed her long jet hair, yanked hard as Suni rolled, pulling her over, ignoring the pain. He was running full speed as Suni got hold of Sally's hand, bit down on it, and he heard Sally's cry of pain. The Indian girl rolled again, landing half atop her opponent, avoiding Sally's clawing hand that just missed her face. He reached the clearing just as Suni's hand reached for Sally's throat, and he grabbed Suni by one arm, yanked her back, and flung her to one side. Sally had rolled over, was starting to get up when his foot caught her full in the rear to send her sprawling forward onto her face.

"That's enough, goddammit," he yelled. Suni rose, her face dark with fury, started for Sally, but he reached out, yanked her to him. "No, dammit, *no*." He shook her. "*No!*" He flung her away and turned to Sally, who'd gotten to her feet, face reddened, one hand rubbing her rear as her eyes flashed fire at him.

"Bastard," she flung at him. "She started it."

"Not really," he countered.

"I'm not taking orders from her," Sally said hotly.

"Why? Because she's an Indian? Go on, say it," Fargo thundered.

"No, because I'm your prisoner, not hers," Sally shot back. It was an oversimplified answer, Fargo realized, but decided to accept it for what it was. She wasn't even aware of the reverse possessiveness in it, he wagered. He turned to Suni, saw she'd come up close, the black-brown eyes burning with silent rage. He had to make a quick gesture, he knew, something to defuse the seething rage inside the Indian girl. He turned back to Sally, pulled her forward by one arm roughly.

"You do what Suni tells you to do," he rasped at her. "That's an order, you hear me?" Sally's eyes spit sparks at him and her pert face had gone pale white. He shook her by the arm. "You understand, dammit? Answer me," he boomed.

She swallowed hard. "Yes," she murmured through lips that hardly opened.

He flung her backward. "Now start cleaning those pelts," he said to Sally, turning to Suni. The dark rage in her eyes had lessened and he saw the hint of satisfaction around her mouth.

"Suni cook hares," she said, and he nodded agreement. He followed her into the house, took her by the shoulders, spoke firmly but softly.

"No more fighting. No more," he told her, and she agreed with a flick of her eyes. He put the carbine away, looked to the horses in the lean-to, and checked the feed that had been put out for them. When he returned to Sally, she had just finished the pelts and he took them from her as she rose to her feet. Her eyes managed to look hurt and furious at the same time.

"Is humiliating someone another of your pastimes?" she bit out.

"Humiliating? Is that what you think I was doing?" He frowned.

"You've a better name for it?" she snapped. "She hit me first."

"Yes, I've a better name for it. Trying to save your damn neck," he threw at her.

"I was holding my own. I can take care of myself," she flared.

"You were lucky I got here," Fargo said.

"If she comes at me again, I'll scratch her face to shreds," the girl glowered.

Fargo shook his head in exasperation, his voice low and made of steel. "Dammit, you're out of your league. You won't be in some sorority clawing and hair-pulling match. You back down from Suni if you want to keep your head on. She'll simmer down in time," he said, and hoped his words were more than just words. "I'm doing my best to soothe her. She's important to me," he said.

"Of course," Sally snapped. "I wouldn't want you denied your pleasures every night."

"I'll remember that," he answered, started to turn away.

"You're disgusting," she flung at him.

"Maybe. But satisfied," he said mildly.

"It's just animal pleasure," she called out.

He turned, gave her a mild glance. "Something wrong with that?" he asked, saw her cheeks grow red.

"There's no civilized emotion," she said.

He let his lips purse. "Civilized emotion," he repeated thoughtfully. "Such as playing coy, lying, calculating, being all tied up in knots inside?"

"Such as caring," she returned. "There's no caring."

"I wouldn't be so sure about that," he answered

as he walked from her. He went into the cabin, saw Suni had the hares cooking, and watched her add some toothwort from the night before. Sally finally came inside as night rolled over the mountains. The meal was eaten in silence and he was not unaware of Sally's quick glances at the Indian girl. Suni had taken off the little vest as she ate and Fargo smiled inwardly. Sally's glances carried grudging admiration as well as disapproval in them. When Suni took the iron kettle out to clean it, Fargo rose, unbuttoned his shirt, stretched.

"Better get your curtain up. I'm turning in early," he said.

Sally flashed a look of tolerant pity. "It must be a burden to be so consumed with lust," she said.

"Not any worse than being consumed with jealousy," he answered, saw her mouth drop open, and then she swung, an arc of her hand. He blocked the blow easily.

"Bastard," she hissed.

"Temper, temper," Fargo chided.

"I'm not jealous," Sally glared back. "Certainly not of her."

"Maybe you ought to be," he commented.

"Why?"

"Because she's honest," he said coldly. Sally spun away, scooped up an armful of pelts, and began to hang the curtain. Suni returned to envelop him as totally as the darkness enveloped the small room, and later he lay awake, thoughts turning to the end of the summer. Only a few weeks left. They'd be coming to buy furs then. He had no doubts how it would turn out. He only wondered how Sally would take the truth. Not well, he was certain. She believed in her brother. Craig Bowers carried all the older-brother worship of a younger sister, had probably basked in it for many years. But she believed in his innocence. Because she knew him so well or because she didn't really know him at all, Fargo pondered. Blind faith was often far stronger than experience. He thought about ways of drawing her out more on Craig Bowers. It'd be difficult. She was too quick-witted to trick into admissions. Fargo turned on his side. She'd still be a problem. He expected that as he dropped off to sleep, but not the kind of problem that came with the morning.

He was outside preparing to visit the trap lines, Suni getting the horses, when Sally emerged, and he felt his eyebrows go up. She wore only a slip that reached just above midthigh and clung everywhere else. Her legs were long, finely turned, a doelike loveliness to them, narrow hips under the clinging slip, a tiny waist, and as she moved, the saucy breasts pushed up against the very top of the slip with piquant provocativeness. She'd none of the full, deep womanly beauty of Suni's figure, but it was a contrast of loveliness. She sparkled with her own kind of beauty. He saw the enjoyment in her eyes at the surprise on his face. He saw Suni returning from the lean-to with the horses, stepped closer to Sally, growled out his words.

"What the hell do you think you're doing?" he asked.

Her brows rose in mock surprise. "Just getting some sun," she remarked.

"Hell you are," he growled back.

"Since when do you object to the beauty of the female form?" she asked tartly.

He cursed silently, understood it at once for what it was, playing games, striking back at him, partly for his nights of enjoyment and partly because he'd stung deep at her yesterday. His eyes flicked to Suni. The Indian girl had halted, her eyes on Sally. She read the girl's appearance with a different understanding. In the black pools of her eyes he saw the instinctive female understanding of a threat, a challenge on that most basic of all levels, the sexual one.

"Suni doesn't know about playing games," he said tightly. "You're asking for trouble and I don't want trouble."

"I'm just being honest," she said sweetly.

"Like hell," he barked, spun on his heel, and motioned for Suni to follow. He strode into the woods, slowed for Suni to catch up with the horses. When they reached the traps, he found two had been sprung, the bait taken, and a third pulled out of place. Wolverine, he reckoned. He had Suni cut some more bait with the hunting knife she wore on the thong around the waist of the deerskin dress. When she'd done so with quick, deft strokes, he restocked the traps, covered the man scent on them with more musk oil.

Suni usually chattered as they worked, leaned herself against him much as a kitten curls around one for petting. This day she worked in utter silence, kept distance between them, and he could feel the simmering anger of her. Finally he went to her, kissed her breasts after lowering the top of her dress, held her close. She wriggled free, lay down on the grass for him with a passive obedience. She was his, her eyes said. He could do what he wanted with her. He swore inwardly, pulled her to her feet. Neither fondling nor screwing would reach her, tell her anything, he realized. Not now. She had seen him taking in Sally's figure. But more than that was the challenge Sally had flung down, the use of her sex the Indian girl understood only one way. Damn, he had to give it a try, he told himself, took Suni by the shoulders, and made her face him.

"She is playing," he told her. "She plays games." The black eyes glowered, didn't so much as flicker. He made the Sioux sign for children. "Playing," he said again, and knew he wasn't reaching her. He took the tip of her hunting knife, drew a child's figure in the dirt. "Playing," he said again.

Suni's eyes didn't change, but she spoke, her voice flat. "Woman. She is woman," Suni said coldly.

Fargo's mouth tightened. She was right, of course. Sally was no child, and therefore she was not playing games. Women didn't play games. Damn, he swore inwardly. How could he tell her about a culture where

97

some women played games all the time? How could he make her understand a kind of behavior that had no counterpart in her world? He gathered breath and tried again.

"She doesn't want me," he said, using words and sign language. "She not want Fargo."

Suni's face did not change expression. "She want Fargo," her voice answered with absolute flatness.

He wondered for an instant at the insights of feminine instinct, and he shifted approaches. "Well, she won't have Fargo," he said. "Understand? She won't have Fargo."

Suni's eyes didn't flicker as she answered, her face impassive, "She not have Fargo."

"That's right." He smiled quickly. "She not have Fargo."

He searched the girl's black-coal eyes to find reassurance that he had indeed reached her, that she understood what he was saying. He found only a liquid curtain and felt a wave of uneasiness sweep over him. The barriers of cultures, he told himself, and hoped he was right. He took her hand, held it as they walked back to the cabin through the afternoon sun.

Sally hadn't changed her outfit and that didn't surprise him. But she had sorted all the pelts, making separate piles of beaver, otter, red fox, snowshoe hare, and all the others. It was a task he knew had to be done sooner or later. "Good," he said brusquely.

"Tomorrow I'll arrange each lot by quality and size," Sally said amiably. "Gives me something to do. I have the water in the kettle heated."

Fargo's glance flicked to Suni, saw her lead the horses to the lean-to, her high-planed face as if carved in stone. When she returned, her eyes passed over Sally with a curtained, deliberate slowness, and Fargo felt the uneasiness stab at him again. He followed her into the cabin, stroked her hair as she added pieces of meat to the kettle. She gave no sign that he was even there, and he turned away as Sally entered with an armful of the sorted pelts. He started to move to help her, checked himself as he felt Suni's eyes on him. He sat down against the far wall and watched Sally carry in the other stacks, depositing each one with a smile of contained smugness and a quick flicking glance at Suni.

"See how handy I can be?" she remarked pointedly. Fargo's eyes watched her with cold anger and he cursed her bitchy little hide silently. The meal was ready by the time she'd carried in the last stack, and he found her sitting down close beside him, in a position where he couldn't help but notice how her up-turned breasts pushed tight against the top of the slip. Suni, wearing the deerskin dress, sat across from him and ate in silence, using her hunting knife to cut the larger bits of meat apart, her face an impassive mask, her eyes hardly moving yet missing nothing. The meal finished, he rose, took the heavy iron lid from the kettle, and began to carry the still-hot pot outside to empty and clean it.

"I'll help you," Sally said, rising as he neared the door. She'd taken only a single step when Suni, uncoiling like a steel spring, leaped in front of her, blocking her path. Fargo started to set the kettle down when he saw Sally smile, a quietly pleased, thoroughly bitchy smile, half-shrug, and turn away. Suni remained motionless for another minute, then turned and followed him as he walked from the cabin. She helped him clean the kettle in silence and he wondered if all his efforts to reach her that after-noon had really worked.

Sally had the fur curtain up when he returned to the cabin. As the room grew dark quickly, the fire burning low fast, he watched Suni remove her hunt-ing knife and the leather thong on which it hung at her waist, then pull the deerskin dress from her head, stand for a moment looking down at him, and in the deep liquid eyes he thought he saw pride and fury, passion and dark resolve. Of them all, he was certain only of the passion as she lay her full-breasted coppery body over his and pulled him into her with silent fervor that reached new intensity.

When it was finished, he lay back, catching his breath, and her arms circled his neck, her face against his cheek. "She not have Fargo," he heard her whisper, and he breathed a sigh of relief. She had understood in the afternoon. He slept as she curled up beside him.

6

He woke first in the morning, dressed and went outside, decided the pinto needed a brisk rubdown. He was just finishing when Suni came out, the deerskin dress on, the hunting knife at her waist. She brought him coffee, her face impassive once again. "You do not smile anymore," he chided her. "I don't like that." Her eyes bored into his, too deep to read. "After yesterday, after last night, I thought you would smile again."

Her face didn't change. "Suni smile soon," she said.

"Good," he said, smiled at her reassuringly, and wondered if he'd ever be able to really read those seemingly bottomless eyes. Certainly never in the few weeks left, he knew. He turned as Sally came from the cabin. She wore only the slip again, but she carried a deep-blue towel in one hand and radiated a sparkling, vibrant loveliness. She was still playing her casual, airy role, he saw at once, giving him a coolly provocative glance as she halted, flipped the towel over one shoulder.

"Where do you trap?" she asked.

"Mostly along the upper reaches of the stream," he answered.

"Then I'll go downstream. I feel like a dip in a cool stream and then a bit of sun in the woods, and I like privacy when I do that," she announced airily. "I'll finish sorting the pelts when I come back."

She moved off at once, tight little rear swinging beneath the clinging lines of the slip.

"We go now," he heard Suni say.

"Yes," he agreed. "Take the horses," he told her. With Suni following, he moved upland to where the stream broadened, flowed more swiftly, and where the beaver and muskrat gathered. The trap line followed the stream's path and he had carefully marked the location of traps placed beneath the water. He found two muskrat and a gray fox, set about to remove the animals and skin them. All summer he'd been playing trapper and the distaste was still inside him as he set about the task with grim efficiency. He glanced up, to see Suni standing by the horses, making no move to help him as usual. He returned to his task, glanced up a few minutes later, saw the horses tethered to a low branch. "Suni?" he called. There was no answer.

He stood up, moved, peered around the horses. She wasn't there. "Suni?" he called again. Only the silence answered. He felt the frown slide across his forehead as he slowly scanned the trees. She had vanished, noiselessly as an Indian, he grunted wryly, and suddenly the silence shouted at him. Suddenly the silence was full of words—her words—that came flooding back to him wrapped in new meaning. *She not have Fargo.*

"Jesus," he swore aloud, bolted like a scared buck, leaped over a log, and plunged into the middle of the stream. Splashing water on both sides of the low banks, he ran down the stream as he swore at himself, at Sally Bowers, and at most everything in general. Except Suni. She was acting in the way that was part of her ways. His foot slipped on a wet rock and he went down on one knee, swore, leaped forward again. The stream took a slow curve to the left and he'd reached the end of the turn when he heard the scream, Sally's voice.

"Oh, God," he groaned as he leaped to the dry ground. She screamed again, more pain in her voice

102

this time, and he saw the flash of figures just ahead, plunged through a thicket in time to see Suni on top of Sally, the hunting knife upraised. Sally's hand gripped her wrist, trying to hold the blade from plunging into her, but she was no match for Suni's strength. Fargo dived as he saw the blade come down, flung one hand out, and struck Suni's arm. The blow was just enough to deflect the knife as she slashed down with it, and he saw the blade go into the ground a fraction of an inch from the other girl's neck.

Suni brought the knife up again to strike, but he yanked her back, rolled with her, and she surprised him with her strength as she pulled free, twisted away, and leaped to her feet. Her black-coal eyes saw only Sally, and she started around him, the blade raised. He stuck a leg out, tripped her, and she went down on one knee. His blow was flat-handed but with force behind it, and it caught her alongside the temple. She toppled sideways and he was on her instantly, wrestling the knife away from her. He flung it aside into the brush, yanked her head up by the long black hair. "Stop it, dammit," he shouted. "No more. Stop it!" Her eyes were still twin black fires raging out of control, and he slapped her again, less hard this time. "No," he shouted once more. "*Stop!*"

She blinked and he shook her; she blinked again and slowly he saw the rage begin to recede in her eyes. He watched as she focused on him and saw the tight fury of her face soften. Slowly, her lips parted and she began to get to her feet. He reached out, helped her up. "You stay here," he ordered as he turned, strode in two long steps to where the other girl lay on the ground, her face drained of color. A line of red trickled down her left thigh, another from a slash across the side of her abdomen. He knelt down, examined both marks, and breathed a sigh of relief. Both were superficial. "You were lucky," he told her grimly.

"She just came at me from out of the trees," Sally

said, gasping, and he felt the trembling of her body as he helped her to her feet.

"Can you stand?" he asked.

She put weight on both feet as he supported her with one arm around her slender waist. "Yes, I can make it," she said. The red line grew stronger as she stood and he pressed the slip tight against the cut.

"You'll be all right," he said. "I've some Gilead salve in my saddlebag at the cabin." He turned to Suni.

"Wait here for me," he said. Her eyes met his, deep whirlpools of racing emotions, and then she bolted, flinging herself into the woods, leaping across thickets like a frightened doe. "Suni, no," he called at once, but only glimpsed her form flashing through the trees. He took his arm from Sally, shot a quick glance at her. "You can make the cabin alone. Just keep the slip tight around your leg. Get the salve, rub it over both cuts, and bandage them with pieces of your petticoat."

If she gave an answer he didn't hear it as he raced into the woods. "Suni," he called. "Come back. It's all right." He shouted again as he ran. "Suni, come back." He felt his lips pulled tight in bitterness. She was fleeing with remorse, fear, guilt, and the thought that he wanted only to punish her. He had saved Sally, come to her rescue. What more proof did she need in her world of simple codes and uncomplex rules?

"Suni, dammit, come back," he shouted again, slid to a halt. She wouldn't heed his call, not now, and blindly running after her was useless. She knew how to flee through the woods with the silence of the deer. The wilds were her home. To catch her required his trailsman's wisdom. He moved forward on the balls of his feet, ears tuned, his eyes scanning the leaves until he found what he sought, twigs broken off at their tips, leaves still brushed backward. He broke into a fast, ground-eating trot, following the trail of leaves slowly springing back into place, patches of grass still pressed down.

She was moving quickly, using only silence to flee, making no effort to cover her trail, and he was grateful for that. She was running down the slope heedlessly, unaware he was in pursuit. The demons of her own inner torment were enough. He moved on long loping strides, his pace more controlled, and he knew he was gaining on her. The grass where she stepped lay flatter, pressed down but minutes before, and the brush in the thickets hadn't bent back hardly at all. He halted, spotted a brushed-aside passage where she'd changed directions, and he followed, quickening his pace. He spied a cluster of orange milkweed pods bruised and crushed as she plunged through them. She'd changed direction again, now moving horizontally across the mountains, still in headlong flight. Fargo's long strides continued gaining on her when suddenly he heard two sounds at once, her scream perhaps a fraction of a moment before the earth-shattering roar.

It was a roar he knew all too well, the deep, thunderous, snarling roar of a grizzly, a sound unmatched by any other creature. As he raced forward, she screamed again; the scream was followed by another angry snarl, and he heard the brush being broken, swept aside by the bear's ponderous form. Fargo skidded to a halt, almost fell, but saved himself by clutching a low tree branch as the ground suddenly fell away in a deep pocket. Below, he saw the black-brown giant rearing up on his hind legs, at least ten feet in height, a tremendous roar filling the little hollow. Fargo's eyes swept the scene, saw Suni, the deer-skin dress a flash of tan amid the green. She was on one knee behind the trunk of an oak. Still reared up on his hind legs, the giant bear marched toward the tree.

Fargo quickly saw what had happened. She'd tumbled into the hollow, as he almost had, and the grizzly had been there. She'd escaped instant death only because the huge bear had been taken by surprise. As he watched, Fargo saw the grizzly drop to all fours, move forward with the speed that never failed to surprise the unwary. The bear swiped out with one giant paw, curling it around the side of the tree trunk, and Suni fell back, twisted, started to run. The thickness of the underbrush caught at her legs and the grizzly was around the tree in seconds, lashing out with a tremendous blow that fell short only by inches. Suni flung herself sideways, rolled to the right, but Fargo saw the bear spin his huge form with amazing agility.

The girl could avoid those crushing paws only for a few seconds more, he knew, and even that vanished as she slipped and fell. He saw the terror in her face as the grizzly reared up on his hind legs again. Fargo drew the Colt and fired two quick shots into the huge furred body. They were fired only to distract the bear with a moment's pain. Only a heavy-duty carbine could bring down a grizzly. He saw the bear shake his huge head, let out another roar, pause for a moment, then return his attention to Suni. "Damn," Fargo swore, fired another two shots. The grizzly roared again in rage, half-turned, dropped to all fours, his little eyes seeking this new annoyance. As Fargo watched, the grizzly scanned the bottom of the hollow, found nothing, and swung back to Suni with the single-minded purposefulness that was characteristic of the giant killers.

Fargo swore again and shouted, dug his heels into the earth, and let himself slide down the steep side into the hollow. This time the grizzly turned fully around, focusing on the intruder. Fargo got to his feet, felt his mouth go dry as memories rushed back over him. The bear-claw scar on his forearm began to throb. He'd been lucky last time. He'd need more than luck this time. The grizzly's mouth opened and the red gums flashed, above them the glint of fangs as long as a man's finger. Fargo gripped the Colt that had only two shots left in the cylinder. Two bullets, and both all but useless. The handgun hadn't the power to penetrate the huge body in a vital spot and the thick bones of the great skull formed a shield of their own. There was one chance only and he'd have but one opportunity to take it.

He saw the giant bear begin to move toward him, a swaying, lumbering gait that, he knew, could turn into astonishing speed. Fargo moved slowly to one side, his eyes flicking to the brush, to where Suni had pulled herself to one knee, her deep eyes wide with terror. The grizzly shifted direction with him, starting to gather speed. Fargo kept moving to one side, retreating at the same time, his glance flicking from the bear to the surrounding terrain. Suddenly he spied what he sought, the green mound of moss covering a rock that jutted out of the ground. He fixed its position in his mind, moved toward a tree near it.

With a shout, he suddenly bolted for the tree. The grizzly reacted instantly, the tremendous bulk shooting across the ground to cut off the racing figure. Fargo saw the huge head coming into his line of vision as he raced for the tree. It would be closer than he wanted, and gathering his leg muscles, he dived the last few feet. He felt one huge paw sweep the air as he landed back of the tree. The grizzly brought his two-ton form to a halt and Fargo used the precious few seconds to scramble over the top of the rock, come down behind it. By the time he turned, the grizzly was charging again, this time in a straight line.

Fargo hunched down behind the rock, not for protection, which was impossible, but to steady his hand. He aimed the Colt at the onrushing mountain of fury, saw the bits of slaver flying from the open jaws. He counted off split seconds, forced himself to hold his position. The huge skull filled the gunsight, and he shifted aim, peered directly at one glittering beady eye, so small for an animal of such bulk. The grizzly started to rise up. Fargo lifted the Colt, keeping his bead on the bear's left eye, the one path to the brain, his single chance for survival. As the grizzly paused for that split second before swooping down with the crushing paws and ripping claws, Fargo fired both remaining bullets, one directly after the other.

He flung himself backward, rolled, came up against another tree. The huge bear was still up on its hind legs, its giant jaws hanging open. Fargo licked lips as dry as sunbaked driftwood. The huge form moved, took one step toward him, then one more. Fargo steeled himself for the crushing, ripping blow of one huge paw when the tremendous body shuddered and pitched forward, to land across the rock, one mammoth paw outstretched almost to where he lay against the tree. Fargo felt the throbbing of the bear-claw, half-moon scar on his arm as he pulled himself slowly to his feet.

He swallowed through a throat parched of liquid, moved around the mountain of brown fur, to see Suni standing at the other side of the little hollow. She saw him and began to run toward him, flung herself against his chest, crushed herself in the circle of his arms. Finally she looked up at him, the deep liquid eyes filled with gratitude and incomprehension.

"Fargo come to save Suni. He fight for Suni," she murmured. "And he save her. I not understand."

Fargo's little smile was tight and he spoke as much to himself as he did to her. "No, of course you don't understand, and it's more than I can explain to you," he said. "Different worlds make people act in different ways, sometimes better, sometimes worse." Her eyes continued to question and he took her face in his hands. "Hell, maybe I did what I did as much for myself as for you," he muttered. "It doesn't matter. It was done and you understand that much of it. That's all I wanted."

He saw her little frown as she struggled to follow, to take meaning of his words. He smiled at her, took her finger, and touched it to her breast. "Understand from here," he said, moving the finger to her forehead. "Not from here."

She stared at him for a long moment, and then a slow smile formed on her lips and she pressed her head against his chest. He held her, waited. There was more to say. He couldn't take her back to the cabin. It wouldn't work, not even after this. He'd wanted her with him when Craig Bowers sent his men out buying furs again, but he'd have to go it without her. She'd never stand still for the challenge Sally posed and she would have to meet it again in the only way she knew. Hell, he'd neither the time nor the taste for trying to teach a course in the ways of the white man's civilization.

He took her hand, sat down on the ground with her. "I'm going to take you back to your people," he said, and her eyes questioned at once. "No, not because of her. Not just that," he answered. "Remember, I told you once that I'd leave the mountains when the summer ends?" She nodded gravely. "I'll be going to places full of people, towns, villages, maybe far away. You'd not like that."

She frowned, thought seriously for a moment. "No, I not be happy in those places," she said.

"Your home is here, with your people," he said. "It's best that way. I'll take you home." Her eyes held his, an infinite sadness suddenly swimming in their dark depths.

"Yes," she said slowly. "It is best that way."

He rose, pulled her up with him. "We'll get the horses," he said.

She walked beside him in silence, holding on to his hand, until he'd retraced his way back along the stream bed to where the horses were tethered. He returned to the cabin for two reasons, one to get his saddle, the other to talk to Sally.

"I wait here," Suni said as they reached the edge of the clearing. He saw the instant hate spring back into her eyes and knew he had made the right decision. He led the pinto to the cabin, saddled the horse, and then stepped into the single room. Sally sat against a pile of the pelts she had put down near the fire.

Pieces of a petticoat bandage covered the cut on her leg and the salve was spread across the smaller cut on her abdomen. The top of her slip was rolled up to cover her breasts.

"Did you catch her?" she asked at once.

"Yep," Fargo said, and Sally's eyes waited. "She's outside," he added.

The girl's eyes widened with instant fear and surprise. "You brought her back here?" she protested.

"Just to get my saddle. I'm taking her back to her people," he answered.

"I don't know why you went chasing after her in the first place," Sally commented.

"You asked for what happened," he said coldly.

"I didn't think she'd try to kill me," Sally said.

"You didn't think. Didn't listen to me either," he snapped. "You were too busy playing games. I'll be back sometime in the morning."

Her eyes widened. "You're leaving me here alone overnight?"

"Yep," he said, turning to go. "You can take care of yourself, remember?"

She shot a quick glare at him. "Then give me my gun," she said.

His smile was hard. "No dice. The door bolts from inside. You'll be safe in here."

"I'm sure she can find her way back by herself," Sally protested acidly.

"Your bitchiness is showing," Fargo said.

"She tried to kill me. What was she showing, dammit?" Sally flung back.

"Honesty," Fargo said softly. "The kind you don't understand in your world."

"Isn't it your world, too, Fargo?" she speared.

"Yep, and there's not much I can do about that," he said. "We're stuck with the cards we've been dealt." He pulled the door closed and strode to the pinto, swung into the saddle, and rejoined Suni. She rode mostly in silence on the long journey across the ranges of the Wind River Mountains, and it was nearly dark when they reached the Ponca campsite. Guards led them into the camp and the Ponca chief emerged from his tent to greet them.

"I bring Suni back to her people. Soon I will be going on," Fargo said. "It is best for her to be here. This is her home."

The old man nodded gravely. "She has pleased you?" he asked.

"Very much," Fargo said.

"You will come to us again one day?" Tantowa asked.

"Yes, one day," Fargo said. Suni turned with him. "Walk to the edge of camp with me?" he asked, and she nodded, her face quiet. "Smile once more for me," he said as they reached the dark edge of the camp where the fires lay hidden behind a line of rocks.

"It is hard," she said.

He cupped her chin with his fingers. "Try," he said. "Think of all the good things."

Slowly, her lips parted and she smiled, put her hands against both sides of his face. "I will see Fargo," she said, and he frowned at her. "In the white clouds of the sky, when the waters of the lake smile, when the stream laughs, I will see him."

"And I'll think of Suni often," he said, leaned down, brushed her forehead with his lips. She spun away and ran, vanishing in seconds in the darkness. Fargo swung into the saddle, gathered the reins of the gelding, and began the trip back across the range. He rode slowly in the inky blackness of the night, climbing high into the mountains, finding the stream finally, following its winding way back to the little cabin. It was nearly dawn when he reached his destination, and he was tired. He was angry, too. He'd have to take extra precautions soon or risk having everything go down the drain. All because of Sally Bowers. He swore silently as he put the horses in the lean-to and went to the cabin door, pushed on it, and found it didn't move.

"Open up, dammit," he called. When nothing happened, he pounded against the heavy wood of the door. "It's me," he shouted. Finally he heard her inside, moving around, then the sound of the wooden bolt being pushed back. She opened the door, sleep in her face, the blanket wrapped around her.

"You took your damn time," he growled as he pushed into the room.

"I was fast asleep. I didn't hear you. I'm exhausted," she said, returning to her side of the room, the edge of the blanket dragging behind her.

"That makes two of us," he answered as he pulled off clothes. She hadn't put the curtain up, he noted as he undressed to his shorts, lay down on three of the pelts, and was asleep in seconds. He slept hard during the next few hours, woke when he heard her stirring about. He watched through slitted eyes, saw she had donned a checked blouse over her slip, and he could see the outline of the petticoat bandage on her leg beneath the slip. He watched as she folded the blanket and went to the door, ladled some water from the bucket, and took it outside with her. When she returned, he sat up.

"Make the coffee," he growled.

She turned to stare at him. "Aren't you even going to ask how my leg is?" she said, a hint of petulance in her voice.

"It's fine. I've been watching you," he said. "You were lucky, I told you." He got up, stretched, aware of her eyes on him. "I said, make the coffee," he repeated.

He saw her eyes take on instant fire. "I'm not your little Indian slave girl. Nobody gave me to you to use," she snapped as she walked past him.

He reached out one big hand, clapped it over her rear. "Owl" she yelled as she half-jumped forward. His hand snapped out again, caught her by the arm, and yanked her around.

"You put on that big act," he growled, his eyes blue agate. "You wanted to show how you could com-

112

pete with her. You decided to trade in bitchiness and it backfired. She's gone now, and that was your doing and now you're going to tend the trap lines with me, cook the meals, clean the floors, skin the pelts, stretch and dry them, and do every damn thing she did."

He saw her swallow and the sass go out of her eyes. "I've never skinned anything," she said.

"Maybe you'll learn. I'll decide about that," he said roughly. "Now make the goddamn coffee."

He let go of her arm and she stepped back, turned, and picked up the old, heavy coffeepot. "Because I want to, not because you say so," she muttered.

"Just so long as you do it, that's all I care about," he snapped. He went outside, washed, returned, and pulled on trousers. She had the coffee ready and handed him one of the tin mugs, sat down opposite him. She sipped the coffee and shot an accusing glance at him over the rim of her mug.

"I hardly think you've cause to be so self-righteous about anything," she sniffed. "You were using her as part of your masquerade."

"She came to be part of it," he said. "There's a difference."

"A fine line of distinction," Sally retorted.

"She understood it better than you," he answered. He downed the coffee and got to his feet, took the big Henry carbine from its saddlecase. "Let's go," he said brusquely. "I've got to get dinner when we've finished the trap lines."

She followed him outside, had to take two steps for each of his long strides, but she stayed with him, determination on her pert face, the sharply tipped, upturned breasts bouncing with her every step under the blouse. They were deep in the woods when she threw the words at him, sudden fierceness in her voice. "I hate traps. How's that for honesty?"

"Don't like them either, but you can't play mountain man without traps and a rifle," he answered. "How come you're in with your brother if you hate it so much?"

113

"He buys furs," she said.

"From trappers. Same difference, and you're part of it," he said.

"Only for the past few months," she said.

He kept the edge in his voice, played on the defensiveness that was so near the surface with her. "Don't try to sell me a bill of goods," he growled.

"I'm not. Craig asked me to come out to help him with his office work after I left school," she said.

"How long were you at school?"

"Four years."

"Then you didn't see much of your brother over the past four years," he slid at her.

"Only on holidays," she said.

"Which means you don't really know a damn thing about him," Fargo shot out.

Her eyes narrowed at once. "Very clever," she said tightly. "But I do know him. He's no swindler."

"People change in four months, much less four years," he commented.

"Dammit, you'll see that I'm right," she returned hotly.

"Hero worship," he grunted. "It can hurt bad."

"You're so suspicious you wouldn't know anything about hurting," she said.

"Better suspicious than blind," he grunted as they reached the stream. "Give me a hand here," he ordered, cutting off further argument. He saw her flinch as he brought the first trap out of the deep part of the stream. He did the skinning and had her clean the fresh pelts, and he saw the unspoken gratefulness in her eyes. She was new at it and slow, and it was midafternoon when she was just finishing the second pelt.

"We'll do the upland traps tomorrow," he said. "Keep working. I'll be back." He packed up the rifle and moved into the deep woods on silent steps, passing through the thick foliage without moving a leaf. His first two shots brought supper for the rest of the week, a big wild turkey and a fat quail. When he returned, she'd finished rough-cleaning the pelts. "Take them with you," he said. "You can finish them tomorrow at the cabin. I want to get back. Getting these birds plucked will take time."

When he led the way back to the cabin, he showed her how to help singe the feathers from the turkey as he hung the quail for another day. While she finished cleaning the big bird, he rigged up a wooden spit and positioned it over an outdoor fire. The turkey was roasting over the flames before darkness fell. He sat before the fire, tending the spit; she went inside to return with a shawl, for the night coolness swept down from the high peaks. She settled down near him and he felt her eyes studying him.

"I still owe you," she said. He grunted. "I just wanted you to know I haven't forgotten."

"I didn't figure you had," he said to her.

He felt her hand reach out to touch his arm. "Look, I'm sorry about things. I'm sorry I didn't listen to you," she said.

"Which time you talking about?" he asked.

"Dammit, can't you ever meet a person halfway?" she flared.

"You didn't answer me," he pressed.

Her lips tightened, then loosened. "Both times," she said quietly. "Is that honest enough for you?"

"It's a start," he commented, took his knife, and cut into the turkey. It was done and he cut a piece for her. She ate hungrily, and when the meal was finished, he cut the rest of the bird into pieces to save and to stew. She took the pieces into the cabin as he put the fire out. When he went inside, she was starting to put up her fur curtain. He took down the two pelts she'd hung, met her stare.

"No more of that, honey," he said. "There's no need for it."

"What's that mean?" she asked warily.

He started to take off his shirt. "It means you're staying on my side of the cabin with me," he said.

"Now, wait a second," she began, but he cut her off roughly.

"You threw your little ass around. You got rid of Suni, and I told you you'd do everything she did," he said.

"You wouldn't dare . . ." she gasped out, fear sliding into her eyes now.

"I'd dare," he told her coldly. "Call it another lesson in honesty, if you like. You won't have to toss and turn and wish it were you instead of her."

"I didn't wish anything of the sort," she flung back.

His hand shot out, went around her neck, and pulled her to him. "Didn't you?" he breathed as he crushed his mouth over hers. Her lips stayed tight and he forced them apart, pressed his tongue into her mouth. He felt her push hard against him with both hands, but her mouth stayed open. He pulled back, looked into her eyes. "Didn't you?" he asked again.

"No," she repeated, but this time the word was gasped out, a word stripped of its meaning. He pressed his mouth over hers again, and for another moment she tried to twist her head away and then he felt her tongue move, meet his, push forward. "No," she breathed again as her arms tightened against his. He lifted her, swung her down onto the blanket, and his hand pulled the blouse open. The upturned breasts pushed out at him, beautifully pert, little pink tips rigid against pale-rose tiny areolas. He lowered his lips to each and heard her sharp cry, the protest of pleasure. He pulled gently on her piquant little breasts and suddenly he felt her hands clutching at him, her cries filling the cabin with urgent demandings.

Naked beside her in moments, he pressed himself hard against her and she drew her hands down his back. "Oh, damn, oh, God," she breathed. "Damn you, Fargo, damn you."

He stroked his hands down her abdomen, across the little convexity of her belly, and down through the luxurious mat of dark and tangled threads. He

116

cupped her warm moistness with his hand and again she cried out. He let his hand explore, stroke, caress. "Oh, Jesus . . . oh, please, oh, my God," she screamed, and her head tossed from side to side on the blanket, her hands digging into the fabric. She moved her hips for his touch, the consummate urging, lifted, half-turned, gasped out cries, and with a sudden strength that took him by surprise, flung herself to the side, half over him. Her mouth opened to move down his chest, hurrying across the hard-muscled abdomen and down to the waiting offering. Her lips fell upon him as a parched traveler falls upon a water well, and little cries and murmurs came from her as she worked feverishly on him, almost gulping in his maleness.

Finally she fell back, her breasts heaving as she drew in deep breaths. He turned to bring his body onto her, slowly moved up along her soft thighs as they fell to the side. She screamed as he slid into the sweet darkness of her, held rigidly still for a moment, and then exploded in a frenzy of thrusting hips and writhing pelvis. "Yes, yes, yes," she cried out with each stroke, and once again her head flew from side to side as the pleasure and wanting consumed her, overwhelmed, became more than she could hold on to, contain within herself.

He felt her soft wetness flow around him, and then, with sudden explosiveness, the liquid lips contracted in quick paroxysms. Her legs clamped around his waist and her scream echoed through the little cabin. He held her in that hanging moment as she cried out the cry of woman throughout the ages, victory and defeat, conqueror and captive. Finally she fell back, trembling, her hands still clutching him to her. He stayed inside her and felt the sweet pleasure of the moist glove slowly relax. When he left her, she focused her eyes on him, a little frown furrowing her brow.

"Bastard," she breathed. "Wonderful bastard." She pulled herself up on one elbow as he lay back, looked

117

down at him. "You knew all the time. It was that plain to see," she said.

"You asking or saying?" he returned.

She thought for a moment. "Saying, I guess." Her hand touched his face, brought it around to meet her eyes. "Was that honest enough for you?" she asked.

He nodded, allowed a half-smile. "Was it honest enough for you?" he asked.

She buried her face into his chest. "Yes, more than ever before. Not that there've been that many times," she added. She felt his smile in the dark, lifted her eyes to him. "I didn't need to tell you that, did I?"

He didn't answer and knew she expected none. He watched as she fell asleep across his chest, finally slide down to sleep against his side. Her saucy breasts stayed saucy even in sleep, he noted, pert, upturned, an echo of the quick pertness that was her. She'd been more than he'd expected, the outer veneer shattering in one tremendous explosion. Maybe it would help when that day came, he reflected. Maybe. He hoped so. For all her aggressive tartness she was very vulnerable. He closed his eyes, one arm around her smooth shoulders. He knew one thing only. He'd enjoy it as long as it lasted.

7

He woke with the smell of fresh coffee in his nostrils, sat up to see Sally filling the two tin mugs. She wore a yellow blouse hanging loose outside a skirt that had been cut off to make a variation of shorts. Her smile was bright as the morning, her elfin-cap brown hair tossing as she spun around to face him. She came to kneel down before him as she handed him the mug, and he saw that the blouse was held closed by only one button, her sharp, pert breasts moving provocatively behind the thin material.

"You trying to arouse me, miss?" he asked as he sipped the coffee.

She half-shrugged. "Why not? Two can play at that," she answered. She slid to a sitting position, bare knees curved into dimpled roundness, her eyes studying him. "I once said I almost liked you. I suppose I'd best drop the *almost* after last night," she remarked.

"Don't rush things. You might change your mind again," he answered as he sipped the coffee.

Her face grew serious at once and her brown eyes stayed on him. "No, I won't change my mind again, not after last night," she said.

"No matter what happens?" he slid at her.

119

"No matter what happens," she insisted. "Anyway, nothing bad will happen, I know it."

He grunted and said nothing.

"Last night wasn't something I'll forget," she said. He met her eyes, saw her probing, trying to see beyond the lake-blue eyes that could mask feelings so easily. "I think it's that way with everything about you. You're not a man people forget."

"For one reason or another," he commented wryly.

"Yes, for one reason or another," she agreed with gravity. "Why'd you take this job for Caroline Stanton, Fargo? She's not worth helping. She's a ruthless woman."

He let his lips purse. "Yes, you're probably right about that. I took it for the money she offered," he said.

"I didn't think money was that important to you," she said.

"Not the way it is to some people. But it takes money to keep searching," he told her.

"Searching for what?"

"For the men who murdered my family, everyone in it. They'd have killed me, but I happened to be away. I'll catch up to them one day," he said. "They'll pay."

"Chasing bad memories is no good for a man," she said.

He shrugged. "Maybe," he allowed. He let his eyes find a sly smile. "Only thing worse is chasing women," he said.

"Indeed," she agreed, leaned forward to press her mouth over his. Her hands slid down his chest, moving along the line of his hips.

He grasped her wrists. "There's plenty of work to do today. We didn't see to half the traps yesterday," he told her. "There'll be plenty of time tonight." He rose, washed, and dressed while she cleaned the coffee mugs. She was beside him when he strode from the cabin and into the deep green mountain forests.

"We'll be going upland to the top of the trap line," he told her.

"How do you know where to set the traps?" she asked. "By learning animal habits?"

"That helps, but each animal has its own habits," he answered.

"How do you learn it, by watching?" she asked.

"Sometimes. Mostly by knowing where the animal is likely to go, and that means knowing what it likes to eat. A marten now, he'll only be found in a spot where there are plenty of field mice, rabbits, and chipmunks. Red squirrel is very different. Red squirrel likes the seeds of Douglas fir and pine, but he'll eat a good bit of hickory nut, too. For mule deer you've got to find a good stand of snowberry or jack pine, though when it gets near winter they start working their way down to cottonwood and willow. Now white-tailed deer, they prefer maple, sumac, and aspen, and a good patch of sweet fern will surely bring them."

"It's sort of unfair, isn't it?" she said. "Like lying in wait."

Fargo gave her a stern glance. "I told you once before, fair's only a word up here. Fair is surviving, and that goes for man or beast," he said.

She lapsed into silent thought as they reached the top of the trap line. She worked beside him as he moved along the line of traps, learning quickly, doing much better than she had the previous day. By noon they'd emptied the traps, and by midafternoon, when the sun was at its highest, he'd finished the skinning. Sally found a spot where a wide circle of sun speared through the leafy ceiling to light a thick mound of bright-green star moss. She lay down on the soft bed, basked in the warmth of the sun, sat up, stretched, wriggled out of the blouse, and lay back again on the moss.

Fargo took in the wood-sprite beauty of her, slender legs smooth and fine-lined, the small waist and pert stand-up breasts. He went over to her, looked down at her, and she gazed back out of half-lidded eyes. He saw her arms reach up to him, her hands finding his belt, unbuckling it, slowly sliding his trousers down. She pulled herself up to him, plunging her face between the hard muscles of his inner thighs, lifted her lips, her mouth opening, a tiny sound coming from her, a pleading, caressing sound. He moved a half-step closer, obeyed, and she gasped out in pleasure, pulled slowly on him. She leaned backward onto the soft moss, not letting go of him, and he dropped to his knees with her. Suddenly the quiet glen became a theater of wild desire and the sun-dappled green seemed to envelop him in a blanket of nature.

Afterward, he rested with her in the circled sun, his eyes again marveling at the naked-sprite beauty that seemed so natural in the deep forest. "I ought to leave you here," he told her. "You fit here."

"It's you," she said. "You make me feel free and wonderfully alive, more than I've ever been before." Her eyes grew thoughtful as she studied his face. "You can make a woman unfold, blossom in her own way. That's a special sense, not something you learn how to do."

"Primitive," he remarked.

She didn't flare back. "Maybe more than you know," she said thoughtfully.

"Whatever," he said. "So long as I satisfy. I hate to disappoint anyone."

She lay across his chest, the tips of her breasts soft-hard little points. "Not you, not ever," she murmured.

He took her back to the cabin when the warm sun suddenly vanished.

The days that followed fell into their own pattern, a good pattern. Beneath her tart pugnaciousness, Sally Bowers had a warm naïveté that was undeniably appealing, and each day she seemed more and more a woodland creature. In a totally different way than Suni, though. The Indian girl had been the deep, sensuous warmth of the earth, the magnificence of silent forests, and the surging throb of deep rivers. Sally was sunlight and woodland flowers springing forth, the sparkle of a running stream. Nature embraced many forms of beauty, Fargo reflected. Who was he to do less?

But the days were even more numbered than he'd expected. It was late afternoon and they had just returned to the cabin when it happened. The air turned cold with disconcerting abruptness, a shaft of wind whipping down the mountainside. Sally shivered and hurried inside, and Fargo lifted his eyes to the high cirrus clouds patterning the sky and felt the edge in the air again. The Wind River Mountains had uttered the first soft call.

"A message," he said as he went inside where Sally had lighted the fire. "A sign. Nature always gives signs."

Sally put the kettle on, stirred it slowly. "A message to listen to," she said thoughtfully.

"Yes," he said. "It'll go down the mountains, into every glen and valley."

"And everything will listen to it," she said.

"All the wild creatures will listen. They know. The burrowing ones will take in the last acorns, pull in the last leaves to line their burrows. The deer will feel the wind turn the fur along the top of their backs, and they'll start moving down to the serviceberry and the protected hollows of the lower range. The varying hares will be putting on their white winter coats and the birds will sing a last song before taking off south."

"And one more thing," she said. He didn't answer. "You haven't mentioned that," she pressed.

"Didn't think I needed to," he said.

Her face was set as she stirred the kettle, not looking at him. "How long before they come?" she asked.

"A few days. A few weeks. No telling," he said. "It'll just be waiting now."

She turned from the kettle, faced him, her eyes suddenly flashing defiance, her chin tilted up. "I'm not afraid," she said.

"Good," he returned evenly.

She came toward him, her face set, pulling the blouse off as she did. He fell back onto the blanket with her, and she cried out with a kind of frenzy for all he did and more. The fire had almost gone out when she lay breathing heavily beside him, spent thoroughly. Maybe she wasn't afraid, as she had told him so quickly. Maybe it had been an explosion of defiance, of anger at the reality of the ending suddenly facing her. Maybe. Only he didn't believe her, not one damn bit. She was fighting hard with herself, carrying herself along on brotherly love and hero worship. It was easier when he was the enemy. It let her focus her protectiveness. He found himself half-hoping he was wrong about Craig Bowers as he pulled her against him and slept.

In the morning, she stayed close to him, not unlike a child suddenly afraid but hiding fear by proximity. "I'll be taking the traps in this morning," he told her. "There's no need for any more of it."

"Good," she said. She went with him and helped carry the steel killing devices back, watched as he wrapped them in canvas and tied them. The rest of the day he wandered among the trees that edged the little clearing in front of the cabin as she watched curiously. Finally he found the one he wanted and took the broadax, began to chop away the branches, first the lower ones, then others higher along the trunk.

When he'd finished, he had fashioned a stepping-stone progression that let him quickly climb to a thick branch halfway up the tree, broad enough at the base to form a comfortable seat. From that vantage point, he could see every approach to the cabin. He climbed down, faced Sally waiting below.

"Starting tomorrow, I'll be spending most of every day up there," he said.

"And me?"

"You be here, close to the cabin," he said.

"Am I being a prisoner again?" she said sullenly.

"Not unless you want to see it that way," he told her. "But we'd best get this straight out now. When I see them coming, I don't want you here. I'll signal you and you disappear in the woods back of the cabin and stay there until I come get you."

The sullenness stayed in her face. "I don't see why I can't stay here. You can say I'm your wife."

"Some have already seen an Indian wife here," he said. "And it could be someone who'd recognize you."

Her lips tightened. "It won't be anyone like that," she said.

"So you say," he answered curtly, met the dark anger in her eyes. "You ought to be happy to play along. You want to prove your brother's not back of it, don't you?"

"Yes," she snapped, lifting her chin high. "All right, I'll go along with your way. I'm not afraid."

"I heard that," he remarked blandly. He went into the cabin and she followed, said nothing through the meal. He undressed soon after and lay down on the blanket in the quickly darkening room. When she came over, he saw that she was able to lay close beside him and make it seem as though a wall rose between them. She turned on her side and soon he slept, dimly aware of her restless turning.

He woke first in the morning, brewed coffee, and took it outside to sip the warming liquid. The morning air held its new coolness and he sat down on a stump, waited until he heard her inside, washing, watched as she emerged, her glance going up to the trees as they rustled with the cool wind's promise. She sat down beside him and sipped her coffee. He let her finish, then got up, faced her. "You have it all straight in your head?" he asked sharply.

She rose, eyes still dark with resentment. "Perfectly," she said, started to brush past him.

He stopped her. "I want a promise from you. I want to hear you say it," he said.

She glowered, stayed silent for a long moment. "I promise," she said finally.

He grunted, turned away, and climbed on his step branches with quick ease. He settled down on the thick branch, found the most comfortable position, and began the waiting process. He knew how to wait. He understood what most men never learned: that waiting is just another part of acting. The cougar frozen into stillness watching its prey come into range understands that the waiting is as much a part of the attack as the flashing leap. The red-tailed hawk sitting silently knows the meaning of waiting. Fargo had learned that lesson. Or perhaps it was part of him, rooted in the one-quarter Cherokee blood that ran in his veins. He glanced down, saw Sally standing in the doorway watching him.

"Start bundling up the pelts," he called to her. "There's plenty of rope inside." She nodded, disappeared into the cabin. The task would keep her busy through the day, he knew, and he settled himself against the tree once again. He made a pattern for himself, long slow sweeping movements with his eyes that took in every section of the terrain surrounding the cabin. By the time the first day ended, he had come to know every dip and hollow within his range of vision, and he climbed down only when dusk began to slide across the mountains; he lay down on the ground and stretched cramped muscles until they loosened.

After the meal was over and he began to undress, Sally came to him in the fire's half-light, her eyes still troubled. Her lips pursed for a moment as she chose words carefully. "I've been wondering about something," she began. "This morning, suppose I hadn't promised."

"You did," he said curtly, pulling trousers off. "The rest doesn't matter."

"But what if I hadn't?" she insisted. "What would you've done then?"

"What difference does it make?" he said, wanting to avoid the answer.

"I want to know. I want to know if I was bluffed out," she persisted.

"I don't bluff," he growled.

"Maybe you do," she said stubbornly. "What would you've done, tell me."

"Tied you, gagged you, and tossed you back in the woods out of sight," he told her coldly.

"All day?" She frowned.

"That's right," he snapped.

"Every day?" she pressed.

"Every day."

Her frown deepened and she stared at him, her eyes full of racing thoughts, uncertain believing, wondering, probing. He didn't move, his face made of stone. "Yes, I believe you would," she said slowly.

"Then be glad you promised," he told her.

"You saved my life. Twice. You sleep with me, are kind and understanding to me, let me become close to you. But you'd throw all that aside as though it never happened and treat me like some piece of baggage you hardly know. What's inside you, Fargo? Give me something to understand you," she said.

"I never let pleasure interfere with business," he said blandly.

"That's a surface answer," she rejected with an impatient toss of her head.

He turned to face her fully, and she saw the brilliant lake-blue eyes frost over. "There's right and there's easy," he said, his voice steel. "There's doing what's right, what you have to do, no matter how much it hurts, and there's selling out. There's nothing in between. Most men think there is, but that's where they're wrong. That's where they get into trouble. When the time comes, you've only got one choice, what's right or what's wrong."

"Most people aren't strong enough to live by that," she said. "You can't be something you're not."

"You can try," Fargo grunted.

"You're two people in one, Fargo," she said softly. "One sensitive and one severe."

He pulled her to him. "Just enjoy the one you like best," he said.

Her eyes held his for a moment. "Yes, why not?" she murmured. She lay down over him and proceeded to take his advice.

8

8

Three more days passed with only the quiet movement of the mule deer disturbing the forest. The wind continued to hold its chill and he could hear the mountains growing still as all the chattering, clicking, scurrying sounds disappeared. He had been on his perch most of the morning on the fourth day when his eye caught a new movement up on the high ridge. He shifted on the branch, leaned forward, squinted through the still-thick foliage, and saw the horsemen come into view, moving single file, two of them with a third at least a dozen yards behind. Fargo let a little smile touch his lips. They were playing things very carefully. Two to do the buying, the third one hanging back in case of trouble. His eyes watched the men move into clearer sight. The second one led a pack mule already carrying a load of pelts strapped onto its back. His glance went to the third man hanging behind, saw the carbine carried under his right arm.

Fargo turned on his perch, looked down to where Sally had just finished cleaning out the kettle. "They're coming," he called softly. "Time for you to go."

She looked up at him, held very still for a long moment, and then turned and began to walk around to the back of the cabin. He watched her until she disappeared from sight in the thick woods, and he then climbed down from his perch. He went into the cabin, stayed there until he heard the horsemen arrive outside. He stepped to the door, a wooden spoon in one hand, saw the two men just dismounting in front of the cabin. His eyes flicked to the trees beyond, glimpsed the dark shape of the third man staying back, returned his eyes to the other two men. The first one had a lean, long face with pale-blue eyes. The other one was short, a round stocky body with a face to match.

"'Afternoon, mountain man," the pale-eyed one said pleasantly. "I'm Jeb Dorrance."

"Howdy," Fargo said, stepped out of the cabin.

"Been a good summer?" the man asked. "Get yourself a good haul of furs?"

"I'd say so," Fargo answered, putting the spoon down on a stump. His glance flicked to the trees again, positioning the well-hidden figure in his mind. Just to the right of the big hemlock, he noted.

The pale-eyed man glanced around the little clearing. "We heard you had a squaw wife," he commented.

"She's out in the woods looking for burdock," Fargo said. "Be coming back soon."

"We've come to save you the trouble of carrying your pelts all the way down to town," the man called Jeb said. "We can take them off your hands right here and now."

Fargo made a doubtful face, scratched his head. "I don't know about that," he said slowly. "I figured to sell to the Rocky Mountain Fur folks. I hear they give a fair price."

"That's us, mountain man, the Rocky Mountain folks," the man said heartily. He pulled a square slip of paper from his pocket, handed it to Fargo. "Here's our receipt. See for yourself," he said.

Fargo stared down at the receipt, one of those he'd seen in the box at Manyon's cabin. He squinted at it,

130

held it up to his face. "There's the name printed right on it," the man said. "You see that, don't you?" His voice held a hint of malicious laughter.

"Sure, sure, I see it," Fargo said as the man reached out, took the receipt back from him.

"Well, that's it, then. You get your pelts out and I'll sign the receipt so it'll be all legal, and you'll have your price right here and now," the man said. He leaned the receipt against the smooth seat jockey of the saddle, signed it with a big, showy flourish of his hand.

Fargo went into the cabin and returned with the first bundle of pelts. He made three more trips until all the furs were strapped onto the pack mule. The pale-eyed man handed him the receipt and four bags of gold coins. "No need to count them," he said. "It's all there and in order. Don't lose your receipt," he added, the maliciousness in his voice again.

Fargo looked squintingly down at the receipt, aware of the other man's superior grin. The receipt, signed in an oversized, flourishing scrawl, bore the name "John Smith." He grunted, pushed it into his pocket. As the two men started to mount their horses, his eyes flicked again to the trees. The figure hadn't moved and Fargo measured range and position once again in the split-second glance. He moved to his right, brought his hand back to rest on the butt of the Colt, his legs half-turned to twist on the balls of his feet. There'd be time for but one shot into the trees and then he had to be ready for the two in front of him. The split seconds would tally the result. The two men in front of him started to gather up reins. Fargo kept his tone mild.

"There's just one thing wrong," he called out. The pale-eyed man's brows lifted as he looked at the big black-haired man. Fargo's tone became harsh. "You're two goddamn liars," he said. "You're not from Rocky Mountain."

His eyes darted to the trees, saw the figure start to bring up the carbine. The Colt snapped up, a single shot exploding. Fargo only glimpsed the figure topple sideways, but he heard the crash of the man's body as he hit the ground, snapping off small branches on the way. Fargo was spinning on the balls of his feet as the short, round-faced man drew his gun. The Colt barked again and the short, stocky body half-rose in the saddle, arching backward. The horse bolted and the man's body fell behind the fleeing horse. A hoof kicked up and caught him in the small of the back and a torrent of red spurted up from his chest as though a fountain had been turned on.

The pale-eyed man's hand had started for his gun, held in midair as he saw the barrel of the Colt leveled at his head. He dropped his hand to his side.

"That's much smarter," Fargo growled. "Now get off the horse, nice and slow."

The man obeyed, and Fargo stepped closer, took his gun from its holster.

"Who are you, mister?" the pale-eyed man said, turning to look again at the big black-haired man.

"Fargo's the name, Skye Fargo," he said. He heard the sound at his right, glanced over to see Sally come racing around the end of the cabin. "Dammit, I said stay until I came for you," he said, his eyes back on the man in front of him.

"I heard the shooting," she answered, came forward, her eyes on the man. "Jeb," she gasped out.

"I take it you know this varmint," Fargo commented, saw the man's eyes look at the girl with astonishment.

"Miss Bowers, what're you doing here?" he asked.

Sally glanced at Fargo. "Jeb Dorrance is Craig's foreman," she said, turned to the man again, hands held stiffly at her sides. "Does Craig know you're here, Jeb?" she asked.

The man shrugged. "Wouldn't be here otherwise," he muttered. "It was all Craig's idea."

Sally glanced at Fargo again, her mouth a thin line. His eyes were cold as he met her glance, refusing sympathy on purpose. The best thing now for her was her sense of being cheated, used, and lied to by her brother. She looked back at the pale-eyed man.

He shrugged again helplessly. "Why didn't you warn us?" he mumbled.

Fargo saw her hand come around in a flashing arc, smash into the man's face. "Bastard," she screamed, followed the blow with clawing, ripping slashes of her nails. "Bastard. Liar," she was screaming, exploding into hysteria.

"Jesus," the man cried, fell back, raised his arms to ward off her blows.

"Stop it, Sally," Fargo shouted at her, but she was half-crying, half-screaming. He saw the man fall back again and then, suddenly, she was whipped around and Jeb Dorrance's arm was around her neck, his other hand holding a double-edged throwing knife pushed against her breast. Fargo took a step forward, halted as the man moved the knife upward.

"Drop the gun," the man ordered as he brought the knife up to the girl's throat. Sally had stopped struggling, her eyes round, fear holding her now.

Fargo dropped the Colt on the ground in front of him. "Get back from it," the man said. Fargo took a half-step back. "All the way," the pale-eyed man barked, kept the knife point at the girl's throat. Fargo backed farther, watched Dorrance push forward with Sally, reach down and pick up the gun, keep his hold on her as he backed to his horse. He flung her with one motion, and she pitched forward, stumbled, fell to the ground. Dorrance was in the saddle before she looked up, spurring the horse into a gallop. Fargo exploded into action, leaping across the girl's prostrate form in one bound, racing for the lean-to. He flung the saddle over the pinto, pulled the cinch strap tight in one quick motion, and leaped onto the horse. He glimpsed Sally, still on the ground, half-turned, watching as he raced past her, to disappear into the forest. Fargo could hear Dorrance's horse plunging through heavy brush and he turned the pinto upland to a narrow path that formed a shortcut. When he

133

turned downhill, he emerged only a half-dozen yards behind Dorrance; he saw the man turn in the saddle, surprise flooding his face.

He fired two shots back at Fargo and the Trailsman's lips pulled back in a tight smile. Wasted shots, he grunted, and spurred the pinto on faster. He saw Dorrance glance behind again, fire another wild shot, and then whip his horse on faster. Fargo increased the pinto's speed, kept pace with the fleeing rider, staying just far enough back to avoid offering a clear target. He saw Dorrance whip his horse again. The man was responding exactly as he expected. His horse hadn't the surefootedness for fast riding in the mountains, Fargo knew. Very few horses had that ability, and Dorrance was pushing the horse to its limits. The Trailsman saw the stand of hackberries begin to thin out, counted off seconds. He'd reached ten when Dorrance's horse came to the sudden steep slope.

Dorrance looked back, saw Fargo still in hot pursuit, and plunged the horse down the slope without slowing pace. Fargo reined the pinto in as he reached the top of the slope. Below, Dorrance's horse tried to keep footing but was moving too fast. As Fargo watched, the horse lost balance first and then his footing went. The animal pitched forward as he tried to halt, began to tumble, and Fargo saw Dorrance hurled out of the saddle, his body going into a half-somersault in the air. The man hit the ground with a hard thudding sound as Fargo sent the pinto down the slope in a sideways gait. He reached Dorrance as the man rolled over, came up on his knees, his face scraped and caked with soil. Fargo leaped from the saddle as Dorrance tried to bring the gun up, aimed a straight kick that sent the Colt flying out of the man's hand. He followed with a short looping right, but Dorrance half-fell, half-rolled backward and the blow missed. He tried to follow through, but his feet slipped on the steep slope and he fell. Digging his heels into the ground, he halted his slide, saw Dorrance pulling himself to one knee. He started to rush the man, halted as he saw the glistening knife blade.

He scooted backward as Dorrance came at him, felt with his feet for a piece of dry ground. Dorrance gave him no time, rushed with the knife outthrust. Fargo let his feet go out from under him, landed on his back as the knife blade whistled over his head. He twisted, closed his hand on Dorrance's knife arm, and rolled, pulling the man with him. Dorrance gasped as his arm twisted, and Fargo, using momentum, pulled the arm backward.

"Ow, Jesus," the man cried out in pain as the blade fell from his fingers. The Trailsman brought his left around, smashed it into Dorrance's face, felt the man slide sideways, brought his right around in a tremendous arc. Dorrance went limp, his head rolling to one side along the slope.

Fargo rose, searched the area until he found the Colt, holstered the weapon, and then lifted the unconscious man and laid him across the saddle. He swung on behind the inert form, sat for a minute, and let his breath return to normal, then let the pinto carefully pick his way up the slope.

Dorrance began to regain consciousness when Fargo reached the cabin. The Trailsman's eyes flashed to the lean-to, saw the bay still there. He pushed Dorrance from across the saddle, watched him fall to the ground and lapse into unconsciousness. He swung from the pinto as Sally appeared in the doorway of the cabin. He saw the mixed emotions race across her face as she saw that he had brought back Dorrance. She watched as he bound the man hand and foot with double-knot ties, dragged him across the ground, and tied him to a corner of the lean-to post.

Dorrance regained consciousness as he was being bound to the post, his pale eyes almost colorless now. "You just going to leave me out here tied helpless like this," the man whined.

"If you're lucky," Fargo said. He glanced up at the

135

amount of daylight left. Not enough, he reckoned. The trip to town would take a full daylight's ride. He went into the cabin, stripped to his shorts, and washed the dirt and mud off. As the darkness crept into the cabin, Sally lighted the fire and he saw the redness rimming her eyes. She heated the remainder of the quail in the kettle and he sat down as she dished a trencher full out for him. She slid down to the floor, a shawl of aloneness wrapped around her.

"Eat something," Fargo said.

She shook her head and watched him eat with a silence that accused. He ignored her. It was only after he'd finished that she spoke, her words crackling out. "Don't expect me to be happy with you," she said.

"I don't," he said. "We'll get an early start down the mountain in the morning."

She stared into the fire and he rose, went outside. He went to where the body of the stocky man still lay, dragged him into the trees next to the rifleman. He returned to check Dorrance's bonds and then went inside the cabin. The fire was low, and Sally was still staring into it, the hurting still in her face. He sat down beside her, pressed a hand to her shoulder. "People don't always turn out the way you want them to," he said gently. "Even family." Her eyes turned to him, the pain stark in their depths. "Truth is, you haven't been that close to him these past few years. You said it yourself," he prodded.

She moved her lips before the words came, and then they were slow, each one separate. "I've an aunt, Martha. She always said that Craig had everything given to him and that made him want things too easy. He was spoiled, she said. I never saw that in him."

"You see it now?" he asked.

"No," she said quickly. "There's got to be some reason for this."

"It's called money," Fargo said.

Her eyes became stubborn. "No, some other kind of reason. Maybe he was forced into this by something. Or someone. Maybe he couldn't help himself," she said. He started to tell her how often he'd heard that excuse but checked himself. There'd be nothing gained by hurting her more. "What'll happen when we get back?" she asked.

"Caroline Stanton and her husband will prosecute, I'd be certain," he told her. "Fraud, robbery, and maybe more."

The fire died out and he undressed, lay back, and pulled the blanket over him. She came after a spell, still dressed, he saw, as she lay down beside him. "There's got to be a reason," he heard her murmur before she fell asleep.

"Worship dies hard," he said inwardly, turned on his side, and slept, his arm holding her close.

It was morning when he felt her stir, sit up. He opened his eyes just wide enough to see her go to the fire and pull the iron kettle aside, look inside it. He let his eyes close again, still more asleep than awake, but the hazy image of her by the kettle stayed imprinted like a fuzzy picture in his brain. She had the heavy iron lid lifted in one hand, was turning back toward him. The fuzzy picture suddenly grew sharp. Fargo snapped his eyes open just as she brought the heavy lid crashing down against his temple.

He half-rose, fell back as waves of darkness rolled over him. His head was throbbing, and in the darkness he reached one arm out, tried to grab hold of her. He managed to open his eyes again, forcing them apart for an instant, and then the blackness closed over him again. He heard a voice, as if from some other world, words hanging in space. "I'm sorry, Skye, I'm sorry. He's still my brother." He felt his hands clawing against the dirt of the cabin floor and then the bottomless pit engulfed him.

The sun streamed across the cabin floor when he woke. He felt the pounding in his head, lifted himself half up, and fell back again, lying there for a moment until his eyes cleared. He tried again, made it this time, pulled himself to a sitting position. The pain in his head stayed sharp and he felt his temple, drew his fingers back, and stared at the thin red stain. Gingerly, he felt along his temple. The edge of the lid had broken the skin, but that was minor. The swelling and the throbbing caused the discomfort.

He rose to his feet, swayed for a moment, let his head clear again, and then stepped to the cabin door. Dorrance was there, still bound to the lean-to, but the bay gelding was gone. He lifted his glance, squinted into the sun. Midmorning. He grimaced. She had too long a head start to even think of catching her. "Damn her stubborn, misguided loyalty," he swore softly. Craig Bowers was no damn good. He didn't deserve getting away. Nor a sister as worshipful and trusting as she.

Fargo turned back inside the cabin. She would have plenty of time to warn him, help him run. There was no way to prevent that now, not even any need to hurry. Maybe, when he caught up with her, he could convince her to tell him where Craig Bowers was fleeing. He made a harsh sound at the thought. He wouldn't put bets on that. He went to the bucket, made a compress out of a kerchief, and applied the cold water to his temple until finally the throbbing lessened and the swelling went down some.

He gathered his things, put the Henry .44 into the saddle holster, reloaded the Colt, and went outside. He saw Dorrance's eyes grow wide as he began to saddle the pinto. "You takin' off and leaving me here like this?" the man said.

"I'll be sending someone back for you," he said. "You'd slow me down now, seeing as I've no horse for you."

"Not out here like this," the man protested. "Any damn varmint could come along, a bear or a cougar, anything. I'd be just live meat."

"Possible," Fargo said, tightening the cinch under the pinto.

"That all you can say?" the man asked in fear.

Fargo looked hard at Dorrance. "If it happens, it'll keep you out of jail," he said, swung up onto the

138

pinto, and rode away quickly. He heard the man screaming as he disappeared into the heavy forest terrain. He rode without hurrying, moving down the mountain to the lower ranges. He was still in the grip of the Wind River Mountains when night came, but the land was beginning to slowly curve into flatness. He'd thought long and hard about Sally Bowers as he rode. He'd made a mistake in not figuring she might do exactly what she'd done. She was the kind who didn't let go easy of trust; he should have been more careful. But he made one wager with himself. Bowers would have hightailed it by the time he reached Wind River, but Sally'd be there. It wouldn't be her to run. She'd face the final truth of it and live with the bitter satisfaction of having paid her debt of loyalty. She'd not do more than that.

It was a little before midnight when he reached the edge of Wind River; he circled the town, approached the Bowers warehouse from the back, moved around to the side, and saw the sliver of light coming from the small office alongside the large barns. He dismounted, edged his way along the structures to the lone window of the office. He reached up on his toes, peered inside. Sally was there, sitting in the old chair in front of the old rolltop desk, waiting, her pert face grave. He closed a hand around the doorknob, turned it, let the door swing open as he hung back to one side.

A shaft of yellow light reached out into the dark and a moment passed, and then he heard her voice, "Come in, Fargo," she said softly. He whipped around the doorway, exposed in the light for but an instant, slammed the door shut behind him. "There's nobody out there," she said.

He met her eyes, saw her search his face for a hint of surprise, finding none.

"You knew I'd be here, didn't you?" she said.

"Yes," he told her. His eyes swept over her. She looked very much as when he'd first met her here, another pistol in the holster at her hips, a red-checked

139

shirt pushed out sharply by the upturned breasts he had come to know so well. "You're a stubborn little fool," he said coldly.

Her eyes went to the still-red welt on his temple. "I'm sorry about that," she said quietly.

Fargo's eyes stayed cold. "I'll find him. You can count on that. I don't leave things unfinished," he said.

Her chin lifted. "He's not gone, not run the way you think," she said, and he heard the note of victory in her voice.

"Meaning what?" he asked.

"He wants to talk to you," she said.

"You mean he wants to make a deal," Fargo said.

Her eyes softened. "Please, Fargo, listen to me. Yes, Craig was back of it, but he's sorry about everything. He knows it was wrong, all of it. He said it was an idea that just sort of ran off with itself like a runaway team."

"He tell you all that?" Fargo asked, not hiding the skepticism in his voice.

"Yes," she said. "He wants to make good as best as he can."

"You convince him of that?" he prodded.

"No," she flared. "Though I suppose he saw how upset I was about it."

"Why isn't he here with you?" Fargo questioned.

"He's no fool. He wants a promise. No sheriff, no jail. He said he'll pay back a good part of what he made the last two seasons," she said.

"I'd have to get Caroline Stanton to agree on that," Fargo said carefully, letting softness into his voice. He hadn't put the pieces together yet, but something was wrong. Craig Bowers was a self-centered, small-time polecat. His kind didn't change colors this quick. Fargo's eyes searched Sally's face. Only honesty there, once again. Craig Bowers had lied to her all along, and he was doing it again, knowing she'd buy what he said because it was what she desperately wanted to hear.

140

"Caroline Stanton will go along with whatever you say, Fargo," Sally told him. "We both know that. You're the one that holds the proof."

"I suspect she might," he said mildly.

"I'll meet you here at noon tomorrow. You can tell me then," Sally said.

"Noon," he agreed curtly.

"You see, I was really right all along," she said. "He's not the way you thought. He's no ordinary criminal."

He nodded at the pride in her voice, the triumph and vindication in her shining eyes. He wanted to feel sorry for her, for what he had to do. Only he hadn't time for that. He turned, started to open the door, and felt her hand on his arm.

"I'm sorry about the cabin," she said. "I didn't know what else to do. I haven't forgotten anything, Fargo. Believe me. I still owe you."

"I believe you," he said, and there was no lie in that. He strode into the darkness, swung onto the pinto, and headed the horse toward the main part of town and the Stanton house. When he was out of her sight, he turned off, headed for the open country at the edge of the mountains. He found a place beneath an oak, halted, and bedded down for the night. His jaw was set hard as he fell asleep.

In the morning, he stayed under the tree, brushed the pinto, relaxed until it neared the noon hour. He gathered his things then and rode back to the little office. She was waiting in the doorway as he rode up, the anxiety plain in her face. "It's a deal," he said curtly, saw the deep sigh of relief as her breasts heaved under the shirt.

"I've your word on it, Fargo," she said.

"Your brother comes in with me and you've my word on it," he said. "But I want to hear it from him."

"Of course. He expected that," she said. "He's arranged a place to meet and tell you everything he can do."

"Has he now?" Fargo commented blandly. "Where would that be?"

"A little house that he bought some while back. I'll go to where he is now and we'll both be there tonight, after nine, he said," Sally answered, followed with a quick set of directions.

"After nine, then," Fargo said.

Her eyes turned darkly sober. "I trust you, Fargo," she said.

"Good," he answered, turned, and hurried away before she could say more. As he rode away, he cursed silently those who were so eager to trust and to believe. He returned to the shade tree and stretched out on the ground. The rest was just waiting. He'd no doubts about anything else.

When night came, he rose, his eyes blue ice. He rode slowly. There was no need to hurry, no need at all. He found the rock-filled little river she had told him was the first of the signs, followed it to a two-headed boulder, and turned left to go along a narrow path over a low hillock. The land dipped just as Sally had said, and he rode on another mile or so, halted, slipped from the saddle, and moved forward on foot. Through a line of trees he spied the house in the distance. He left the pinto by the side of the path and went forward, falling into a long loping crouch, moving silently as a big mountain cat. Lights were on inside the house, he saw as he made his way through the trees, halting to drop to one knee. He glimpsed Sally's form passing inside one of the windows; he moved a few yards nearer to the house.

Halting again, he let his eyes move slowly along the line of brush along the nearest side of the house, then swung his glance back to the house. The front door opened up on a small flat area and the thick brush bordered both sides of the ground. He nodded to himself as his eyes again peered into the nearest line of brush. He looked about slowly, very slowly, a few inches at a time, and suddenly he halted. The dark patch formed a kind of black blot amid the brush.

He edged toward it, let it take form, become the back and shoulders of a man on one knee watching the house.

Fargo's hand went down to the leather sheath strapped to his calf, came back with the thin, two-edged throwing knife in his grip. But he'd not risk throwing in the thickly grown brush. He crept forward, almost at the man now, when his foot struck a loose rock. The sound scraped in the stillness and the man whirled, alarm on his face, and Fargo saw the .38 in his hand. He pitched the knife the six inches with the force of a bullet. It sank to the hilt in the base of the man's throat. Fargo's hand closed around the gun before the man could pitch forward on his face, yanking it away before there was the chance it could go off as he fell. He leaned over, lifted the man's head by the hair, and pulled the knife back, wiped it clean on the grass, and returned it to the leg sheath.

He turned, made his way along the brush, circling the house around the back and moving to the brush at the other side of the front cleared ground. He'd been right about the first one, which meant there'd be a second killer waiting. Craig Bowers wouldn't risk it on one assassin. He'd planned it so his victim would be cut down in a cross fire of bullets. Fargo went down onto his stomach, crawled his way forward, mindful of the loose stone that had almost blown it all apart.

The second man was positioned closer to the edge of the brush, his crouching, waiting form easier to pick out. Fargo crept forward on his stomach, inching his way as the man peered out toward the roadway. He neared the figure, staying flattened on the ground, crept within a foot of the man, halted, watched as the man shifted his position. His gun was still in his holster, Fargo saw, allowed himself a grim smile. He pressed his palms on the ground, catapulted himself to his feet. The man half-spun around, eyes wide with surprise, and then Fargo's arm was against his throat, knocking him to the ground. With one hand, the Trailsman yanked the man's gun from the holster, brought the barrel up to press into the man's temple.

"When?" he hissed as he pulled the hammer back, lying half atop the man. "When I ride up or later?"

The man's mouth fell open and he gasped for air. Fargo relaxed the pressure of his left arm on the man's throat. "Later," the man gasped out. "Afterward."

"When I come out of the house," Fargo said, and pressed down again with his arm. The man nodded as his mouth gasped for air. Fargo brought the gun down on his head with all his strength, felt the man go limp at once. He'd stay unconscious for at least a half-hour, the Trailsman estimated as he stood up, threw the man's gun into the trees. He moved from the thick brush and walked to the front door of the house, knocked.

The door opened almost at once, Sally on the other side of it. She reached out, took his arm, and pulled him inside. He looked past her to where Craig Bowers watched. The man was taller than he'd remembered, but his face was the same, an echo of Sally's, the same features but without the strength, his mouth sullen and weak.

"Sally's been telling me about you, Fargo," he said. "I guess it was all over the minute Caroline Stanton pointed you my way."

"Don't know about that," Fargo said. "But it's all over now."

Craig Bowers smiled and Fargo felt himself angering at the falseness in it, deceit and treachery so casually masked. "You pay back most of what you swindled, put two or three states between you and Wind River," Fargo said, acting out his part of the deceit.

"Fair enough," Craig Bowers said. "How much time do I have?"

"Not much," Fargo said.

Bowers smiled again, ruefully this time, glanced at

Sally. "I guess I'm not in a position to argue," he remarked.

"That's right," Fargo said coldly. "No funny business."

"He'll keep his part of it. He promised me," Sally put in.

Craig Bowers shrugged. "Guess we might as well go on into town then," he said.

"I'll take your gun," Fargo said.

"Of course," Bowers said, handing him the .38 out of the holster. He walked to the door, opened it, and stepped outside. Fargo followed him, Sally coming out last, pulling the door closed. Bowers moved to stand by himself to one side. He glanced up at the night sky.

"Feels like winter's in the air," he said.

"Feels that way," Fargo agreed. He watched as Bowers glanced at Sally, then at Fargo, beckoned the girl to him.

"You ride alongside me, Sis," he said as Sally came over to him. She nodded, and Fargo saw the man's eyes gather a frown. He half-turned to the darkness of the brush, looked away again. "Want to get the horses, Sally?" he said, and the girl started across the clearing to where two horses were hitched to a post at the side of the house. Fargo's eyes caught Craig Bowers' hands as they clenched and unclenched, and he saw the tightness coming into the man's face. Fargo, thumbs hooked casually in the top of his gun belt, stood alone in the center of the clearing. He saw the other man's eyes darting back and forth now, watched him run his tongue across lips suddenly gone dry. Sally returned with the horses, brought them to where her brother peered at Fargo with a frown, his hands clenched again.

"You can stop waiting, Bowers," Fargo said mildly. "I told you it was all over."

Bowers stared at him, and the Trailsman saw Sally's eyes turn to him, flick to her brother and back again. "What's going on here?" she asked.

"A change in plans," Fargo said. "There are two hired guns in the bushes. One's dead, the other's out cold. Big Brother had them set up to kill me. You'll notice how he's standing off to the side there. He's been wondering why the hell I'm still standing here."

"No," Sally gasped out. "No, it's not true." He saw her turn to her brother, lips parted, eyes probing, desperately seeking denial. But the tight fury in Craig Bowers' face shattered all but the truth. He spit out the words with cold bitterness.

"You had it all figured, didn't you?" he said to the Trailsman.

"That's right. You agreed to too much too quickly," Fargo said. He glanced at Sally, her eyes still on her brother, and he hated Craig Bowers for what he saw in her face, the death of trust, the rape of worship. "Get on your horse, bastard," he rasped out.

Craig Bowers turned, walked to one of the two horses, started to mount, one leg in the stirrup; then he spun around and Fargo saw the .44 leveled at him. The blanket that had lain over the saddle holster hung turned back now and Fargo cursed silently at himself.

"Drop your gun belt. Very slow and careful," Bowers said.

Fargo unbuckled the belt, let it fall to the ground. The .44 was aimed right at him, the range too close for the man to miss. He saw the cold smile slide across Craig Bowers' lips. "Well, now, I'd say things were going to turn out right well after all," the man said.

"*Craig!*" The name was torn from her throat as Sally stepped forward. "No, you can't. My God, you can't!"

"Shut up, Sally," the man barked. "With him dead there's no proof of anything. I'm home free."

"No, you can't. This is cold-blooded murder," Sally cried.

"Hired guns or his own, same thing," Fargo bit out

as his eyes measured distances, weighed the slender chances. There were none, he saw.

"Please, Craig, no," he heard Sally cry out again.

"Shut up and stay back. This is none of your damn business," Bowers flung at the girl.

Fargo saw him take aim with the gun and he tensed powerful leg muscles. If he were going to die, he'd do it as a moving target. He heard the gun explode as he flung himself sideways, steeled himself for the searing impact of the bullet. He hit the ground, rolled, saw Bowers, his mouth dropping open. Fargo clutched his hands to the ground, stopped rolling as Craig Bowers half-turned, and Fargo saw the left side of his chest turning red. The man dropped to his knees, the gun falling from his hands.

Fargo's eyes turned to Sally. She stood stiffly, the .38 in her hand still pointed at Craig Bowers as he pitched forward to the ground to twitch for a moment, then lay still. She didn't move, her lips hanging open, her fingers as if welded to the trigger. Fargo got to his feet, approached her. He reached out slowly, pried the gun from her fingers. Slowly she looked up at him and he saw the wetness staining her face, her eyes flowing over.

"I don't owe you anymore," she said.

"No, you don't," he told her. He took her arm, turned her around, led her to the horse. She went with him as if sleepwalking, and he helped her into the saddle, climbed up behind her, and rode to where he'd left the pinto. He transferred to his own horse, took the reins of her bay, and led the way back into town. She sat silently, in a kind of shock, he realized. He took a room at the hotel, brought her upstairs with him, and laid her on the bed. He lay down beside her, felt the rigidness of her body. He'd almost fallen asleep when she turned, flung herself against him, and her sobs shook the old brass bed. He muffled them against his chest until, drained, she slept beside him.

He woke first in the morning, went downstairs, and

returned with coffee, to find her up, eyes still rimmed with redness.

"I'll tend to everything, including Dorrance up at the cabin in the mountains," he said.

She nodded slowly.

"What'll you do now?" he asked.

"Go back east," she said. "Relatives, old friends." She paused. "Unless you said to stay."

He held her for a moment and his eyes gave her the answer. "I didn't expect you would," she said.

"When do you want to go?" he asked her.

"As soon as I can," she said with unexpected force.

"There's a stage leaves this afternoon, every Wednesday," Fargo said. "I'll get you a ticket while you gather your things."

"All right. I'll wait for you downstairs," she said.

He left her, hurried to the stageline office in the post-office shack, and purchased the ticket. The single question had been in his mind through the night and he knew he'd have to give voice to it before she left. It came by itself as he gave her the ticket and she waited with the single suitcase, looking so small suddenly.

"What made you do it?" he asked gently. "What pushed you finally?"

She turned her eyes on him, round brown eyes filled with pain they'd carry for too long. "There's right and there's easy, and there's nothing in between. When the time comes, you've only one choice: what's right or what's wrong," she said. "Someone told me that once, a man different from most. He was right."

She lifted her chin and fought back the tears that almost reached her eyes.

He kissed her gently, watched her turn and walk to the stage. She was different than most, too, he told himself. She'd make it on her own. He turned and walked to the pinto, and rode rapidly out to the Stanton place. Caroline was there waiting and flung her arms around him at once.

"How wonderful," she said when he told her it was

148

over, that Bowers was dead. "We can celebrate. Harry's away until Friday." She pulled him down on the leather sofa beside her, her arms still wrapped around his neck. "That little snip of a sister, she was in it with him, of course, wasn't she?" Caroline Stanton said.

She never really knew how she suddenly came to be on the floor on her stomach, flipped over the back of the sofa. All she heard was the sound of Skye Fargo's footsteps, swiftly going out the door.

LOOKING FORWARD!

**The following is the opening section
from the next novel in the exciting new
Trailsman series from Signet:**

THE TRAILSMAN No. 4: SUNDOWN SEARCHERS

*Elbow Creek, Missouri, 1861, a town
that faced everywhere and nowhere—a
jumping-off place for tomorrow—if you
had a tomorrow to face.*

"Get those damn clothes off," Fargo hissed at the girl.

Her deep-blue eyes flashed. "Can't we just get into bed?" she returned.

"No, dammit! It looks right or we're both dead, and I don't hanker for that," Fargo whispered hoarsely. She continued to hesitate and his hand came up, pulled down the front of her high-necked, violet dress. Buttons flew open and the round swell of full breasts pushed forward. She tried to clasp her hand to her breasts but Fargo pushed it aside, yanked at the dress and the rest of it came open. "Get it off, dammit. *Now!*" he demanded.

The girl wriggled her shoulders and the dress fell to the floor. Fargo kicked it under the bed. She stood in her slip, looked uncertain. *"Everything,"* he said fiercely. "They'll be here damn soon." He tore his shirt off, unstrapped the empty gun belt, and pulled off his trousers. She had taken her slip off, then the petticoat under it as he turned in his own nakedness toward her.

The girl stood still for an instant, a magnificent full figure, creamy-white, perfectly rounded breasts, full-thighed legs, a woman's legs, a soft, nicely turned little rear. She dived under the sheet on the bed, pulled it over her as Fargo kicked the clothes under the bed. He reached down, snatched the sheet from her and she gave a tiny gasp of protest.

"You're supposed to be a damn whore, not a schoolgirl," he flung at her. Her eyes darted across his nakedness, blinked, unable to look away from the hard-muscled thighs, the latent power between his legs, the powerful chest and torso. He sank down to her and she started to twist away. His hand yanked her back and he lay half-over her, her warm, sweet breasts cushioned into his chest.

"Wait, they're not here yet," she gasped.

"Wait, hell," Fargo said. He felt her legs, clasped together tightly, muscles tensed. He got his knee between them, pushed hard, and she gasped again as her legs came open.

"No," she murmured.

"Yes," he hissed at her. "And keep them open, dammit." She relaxed for a moment and he moved further across her, lay half-atop her, now. He felt himself stiffening against the soft convex curve of her small belly. Her breasts, deep, beautifully round with large red-brown areolas surrounding tiny pink tips, pushed against him, and her hair, still piled atop her head, gave her a strangely proper sort of wanton beauty. He felt himself growing larger against her, pushing into the soft-wire nap below her abdomen, an arousing sensation, erotically tickling.

One ear listening for a sound at the closed door of the darkened room, he began to move slowly against her, rubbing gently across the dark triangle, not so much deliberate as a reaction, habit making itself felt. "Stop. You don't have to do that," she snapped, her eyes flaring.

"Do what?" he said mildly as he continued to rub against her.

"You know what!" she hissed fiercely.

He lay still atop her, his warmth pressing into hers, exchanging heat with her, and her legs, half-raised, touched the sides of his hips. He shifted a fraction and his hardness lay across the sweet, dark portal. Fargo's lake-blue eyes half-smiled down at the girl. "You're enjoying this, damn you," she whispered angrily.

"Never. I'm acting. Got to make it look good, don't I?" he said.

"Bastard," she breathed at him as he pressed to the very edge of the soft furrow. He felt the pulsation of her abdomen as she drew in deep breaths. His hands held one wrist, the other around her neck while his ears strained for any sound at the door. They'd be here soon, he knew. They were out

there, going from room to room, searching inside the closets
of the empty ones, looking for two figures trying to hide in
some corner. He looked down at her, saw the fear in her eyes
as she lay beneath him, uncertain of him, of everything. He
wasn't too certain of himself. She was a damn beautiful package and he did have to make it look good. The heat of her
was flowing through his loins even as he heard her soft whimpered breath. Still no sound from the door; dammit, he swore
silently.

Why the hell had he gotten himself into this fix? he asked
himself. Plain old-fashioned curiosity and doing good deeds.
A bad combination. The first good samaritan found that out.
It had all started only two short days ago, when he watched
her get off the stage from Kansas City in her high-necked violet dress, looking proper, superior, and quietly beautiful,
and out-of-place as all hell in Elbow Creek. If ever there was
a tumbleweed town it was Elbow Creek, made up of human
driftwood, flotsam and jetsam that stayed only until they decided which way to drift out again. Sitting at a four-way
crossroads, Elbow Creek let a man go into the Northwest
Territory or due west into the savage lands, east back to Ohio
or along Boone's Trace into Kentucky if you could still find
the road, or southwest to the wild territories of Oklahoma
and Texas. Sitting in the lower corner of Missouri, Elbow
Creek was a town with no life of its own, existing solely on
those who passed through on their way to someplace else.

Skye Fargo, The Trailsman, was an intruder here also, here
only because the pinto had sprained an ankle and he wanted
the horse to have a good rest in a clean, warm stable with
plenty of oats. They had that in Elbow Creek, a good stable
and a good whorehouse. They didn't seem to need much
more, except for the excuse for a hotel and the U.S. mail office.

Fargo recalled how he had watched her leave the stage,
carrying only one leather traveling bag. She checked into the
hotel where he'd taken a room for the past three days. Jet-
black hair tied up neatly atop her head, prim, schoolmarm
style, a small, pert nose and a generous mouth, creamy-white
skin made more so by her dark hair. The violet, high-necked
dress couldn't hide a round, full shape; she was a good-looking young woman for all the air of prim superiority she
wrapped around herself. He would have watched her and dis-

missed her, perhaps wondering what brought her kind of girl to check in at Elbow Creek, if it hadn't been for the strange man.

Fargo had spotted him moving to follow her the moment she got off the stage, watched him step into a doorway as she entered the hotel, keeping his eyes glued to the entranceway. Fargo had moved to the other side of the street, casually leaned on a porch post as he took in the man, a thin, tall figure with a bony nose on a tight-skinned face, everything sharp about the face, with a pointed jaw and darting gimlet eyes. The man wore an old buckskin jacket and an equally worn gun belt with a Colt .44 in a frayed holster.

As Fargo watched, the man moved to the entranceway of the hotel but kept to the side, peering in at the girl as she signed the register. He moved back across the street again, settled down to watch the hotel. Fargo felt a little frown crease his forehead, his lake-blue eyes taking in the scene before him. The man was a small-time cowherd, he guessed, or simply a drifter. But he wasn't being idle now. He was keeping tabs on the girl very carefully. Fargo shifted position to the other side of the street as the girl came downstairs and left the hotel. He watched the man detach himself from the doorway and move after her. Fargo sauntered along and saw the girl go toward the small U.S. post office inside the general store. He halted where he could watch both the girl and the man outside. She spoke to the mail clerk and Fargo saw the man turn, leaf through a big wooden box full of obviously unclaimed or waiting mail. After a few moments, the clerk shook his head and the girl left to return to the hotel. Once again the sharp-faced man followed, took up a position across from the hotel, as she went inside, watching from a narrow alleyway between two houses.

Fargo, his curiosity aroused, turned away to walk to the stable, the frown still on his brow. The girl plainly was unaware she was being watched, and by such a low-type. The sharp-faced man had a hard, cruel slash of a mouth, the gimlet eyes of a hired hand who performed anything if paid enough. He was clearly up to no good. Fargo reached the stable, took the better part of an hour to check the pinto, lead-walk the horse for a while and then, with the stableboy, rub the sprained ankle again with a salve of cuckoopint, oil, and sassafras root. He still couldn't get his mind off the girl and the man watching her, and when he finished with the horse he returned to the hotel. The scruffy, weasel-faced figure was still in the alleyway across the street.

Fargo went to his room, stretched out on the hard single bed, stared at the brass bedposts, and finally dozed for a while. He woke to find the night had slipped over Elbow Creek and he rose, softly cursing being stranded in such a town. Another two days at least, he guessed, from the looks of the pinto's ankle during his visit to the stable. He freshened his face from a bowl of cold water on the cracked wood bureau and went down to the hotel dining room, a dim place of not more than a half-dozen tables served by a shuffling old man. The food was ordinary but filling and that was all he wanted. Before he had dessert, he found himself drawn again to the hotel's entrance, stepped outside and looked up and down the single street of Elbow Creek. Idly, he let his eyes flick across to the alleyway. The figure was still there, almost invisible in the darkness, but there, waiting. Fargo stretched casually and sauntered back to the dining room.

The girl entered soon after, sat at a small corner table and ate quickly. He caught her eyes on him once, a level, curious glance, but she looked away immediately when he met her eyes. She walked back upstairs to her room when she was finished with her meal, moving very straight, head held high, the high-necked dress almost masking the fullness of her breasts. She kept her looks well wrapped, even the glistening jet hair drawn up tight atop her head. He finished his own meal and then strolled to the front desk where the register lay open, her name the only new one added during the entire day. *Charity Keller*, the entry read, written in a bold hand, with nothing more after it.

He turned from the book, went outside and began to stroll slowly down the street, stepping aside to avoid an Owensboro platform spring Dray pulled by a team of matched bays. But his eyes had already swept across to the little alleyway and spotted the figure still there. The Trailsman walked slowly on and came to the town whorehouse, the sign over the front entrance in faded, almost unreadable letters: THE HAPPY PLACE. It didn't need a sign, Fargo thought as he noted the two side entrances. Two floors to the building, bar and poker tables on the ground floor. The Happy Place was already going strong, he noted, peering through the ground-floor window. The girls were reasonably attractive. Two stairways, one on each side, led up from the main room to the private rooms on the second floor.

He turned from the window, cut across the main street, and made his way back behind the row of buildings on the other side. His mind continued to stay on the girl in the violet gown, Charity Keller. He turned the name over in his mind. Charity was in trouble and was unaware of it. He walked till he came to the other end of the little alleyway. The weasel-faced man was still there. Frowning, Fargo drifted into the shadows, found a relatively comfortable spot and settled down to wait and to watch.

That's how it had started, a pretty girl getting off the stage and being immediately shadowed, arousing his own damn curiosity. He should have turned away, he thought back as he looked down at the girl lying beneath him, her eyes wide, anger and fear mixed there together, her breasts soft against his chest. He should have turned away then but he hadn't. The sharp-faced man suddenly had visitors, four men on horseback. It had been too dark to see faces but one wore a tan, wide-brimmed Texas hat. They spoke to the sharp-faced man for a few minutes, then rode slowly on out of town.

Fargo moved forward along the wall of an adjoining building, took up another position, and settled down to wait again. Most of the lights had gone out in the windows of the ramshackle hotel, and he decided to follow through on the certainty that had been gathering inside him. He suddenly stepped out into the street, walked into the hotel, and disappeared inside. He went up the stairs, which were almost dark, having only one dim lamp burning at the bottom to send up a flickering gasp of light. But instead of going to his room, he moved to the far end of the hallway and crouched down in the darkness. His lips tightened in a grim smile as, not more than a half-hour later, he heard the careful footsteps coming up the stairway.

The tall, thin figure halted at the top of the steps, peered at the room number on the nearest door, and began to make his way toward the other end of the darkened corridor. He'd plainly stopped to check the desk register too. Fargo watched the figure halt at the last door, take something from his pocket and work on the lock. It wouldn't be hard to open, Fargo knew. The locks on the rooms were little more than a gesture, all old, worn, child's play to slip. In moments, the man had the door open. Fargo rose, watched him slowly push the door in and close it after him.

Fargo was down the corridor in seconds, long legs carrying him in a loping stride. He closed one big hand around the doorknob, turned it as he listened for a moment. There was a single, faint sound from inside, the click of a trigger hammer being pulled back. He snapped the big Colt .45 into his hand as he flung the door open. The sharp-faced man, one knee on the edge of the bed, had his gun pressed to the girl's temple. Fargo could see her eyes open wide in terror. The man whirled in surprise as the door flew open, started to bring the gun up and Fargo fired, one shot that seemed like a cannon in the confines of the room. The sharp-face burst open in a shower of red and the man's body catapulted backward to slam into the brass bedpost, snapping it off. Charity Keller screamed, rolled from the other side of the bed, her light-blue nightgown already spattered.

She hit the floor, looked up, eyes wide with terror. Fargo stepped forward, reached down and pulled her to her feet as he holstered the gun. She clung to him for a moment, trembling, then stepped back, drawing the gown around herself, putting on propriety with surprising speed. Voices and footsteps were nearing in the corridor as she reached out, slipped a blouse on over the top of the nightgown. She was still drawing in deep breaths, Fargo saw, as the door burst open. Three men halted, taking in the scene, their eyes clinging to the faceless form slumped against the wall, the brass bed post bent in half behind him. One of the men was the desk clerk and Fargo saw his eyes turn to the girl.

"He came into my room," she said, pointing to the dead man. "He had his gun at my head when this gentleman burst in."

"I saw him spring the lock and go in," Fargo said mildly. "The young lady's going to need another room for the night. This one's sort of messed up."

"Yes, of course," the desk clerk said. "Number five's empty, just down the hall."

The girl stuffed things into the leather traveling bag and her eyes flicked to Fargo. She'd buttoned the blouse, he noted. "Please, may I talk to you? I haven't had chance to thank you," she said.

He nodded, his face expressionless, followed her as she was

shown to the other room. She closed the door as the des
clerk left with the other two men. "I really have no way t
thank you except with words," she said. "But I am terribl
indebted to you."

"Who was he?" Fargo asked blandly.

Her eyes widened. "I don't know. I never saw him befor
A sneak thief, I imagine. He probably saw me and decided
woman alone would be easy pickings."

"No ordinary sneak thief," Fargo said. "He was on you
tail the minute you got off the stage."

Charity Keller's face remained wide-eyed. "No doubt h
watches incoming stages for likely prospects," she said.

Fargo smiled coldly as he shook his head. "Good try," h
said. "Only it doesn't wash. He never let you out of his sigh
An ordinary small-time thief would've pegged where yo
were staying, then wandered back after dark. He stuck ou
side this place like a shell on a turtle. There's something els
The average small-time thief goes into a room and tries t
take whatever he can and get out without waking anybody
He was pulling the hammer back when I came in. He wa
there to kill you." Fargo paused for a moment, watched he
as her eyes stayed on him, wide, deep-blue orbs revealin
nothing. "Who's after you?" he asked mildly.

Her eyes flickered but she recovered instantly, let a smil
of tolerant amusement touch her lips. "After me?" sh
echoed. "Nobody's after me. He was just an ordinary littl
thief, that's all."

Fargo's eyes hardened for a moment but he let his ow
smile slide across his face. "Sure," he said. "And what ar
you doing in this asshole of a town?"

Her smile grew tighter. "I'm afraid that's a personal mat
ter," she said. She let the smile relax again. "You've come t
my rescue and I don't even know your name yet," she said.

"Fargo. Skye Fargo," he told her.

She extended her hand. "Well, then, Skye, thank you fo
everything," she said, suddenly all formal and proper. "I wis
I could thank you in a material way but I'm traveling on
very tight budget."

"Didn't do it for pay," Fargo said and saw her eyes soften.

"No, of course not. That was rude of me. I'm sorry. Please
forgive me," she said and sounded as though she meant it.

"Have breakfast with me tomorrow," he said.

"Thank you. That would be nice," she said. "About nine? I'd like to sleep late."

"Nine," he said. "Good night." He left quickly, listened as she locked the door after him, let a smile touch his face. She was hiding something. Weasel-face had been no damn sneak thief and she knew as much. He went to his room, undressed, and went to sleep with curiosity still tugging hard at him.

In the morning, he was seated at the table when she came downstairs. She was wearing the high-necked, violet dress again, that air of formal primness wrapped about her once more. "Scrambled eggs and coffee," she ordered. He noticed a faint shadow underlining the deep-blue eyes.

"Have trouble sleeping?" he asked casually.

"Some," she said. "It's a rather new experience having someone's head blown off next to me." The old man brought the coffee first and she took a deep sip of it, her hand trembling for a moment. "I did wonder if you mightn't have just ordered him to put down his gun instead of blowing him in two," she said, faint disapproval in her tone.

"I might have," Fargo said laconically. "But then he might not have. This way I saved both of us a lot of trouble."

She accepted the reply without comment, put on a smile that was just a shade too bright. "Do you spend all your time rescuing your ladies?" she asked.

"Only once in a while," he said.

"What do you do other times?" she asked.

"Whatever interests me. Or pays enough," he said.

Her brows lifted. "No other conditions?" she asked, the hint of disapproval in her voice again.

"Not usually, 'less I set them," he answered. She was a strange combination, beauty kept hidden behind a somewhat severe appearance, a properness that didn't stop her from lying to him about the weasel-faced man. The waiter brought her breakfast and she started to eat.

"That sneak thief last night, he had friends in town," Fargo slid out casually. The fork slipped from her hand and he saw the flash of fright touch her eyes, but once again she recovered instantly.

"I imagine even a thief has friends," she remarked, concentrating on her eggs.

"I imagine so," Fargo agreed. "Where are you from?" he asked.

"Trellisville. That's just south of Kansas City," she said. He watched her eat too quickly, her face suddenly strained. He finished the coffee as she ended the meal, looked at him with another smile that was a shade too bright. "I hope you won't think me ungrateful but I'm going to spend most of the day resting. I'm terribly tired," she said. "Something like last night hits you harder the day after."

"Sometimes," he agreed. She stood and extended her hand.

"Thank you, Skye. I am really most grateful to you," she said, and once again there was honesty in her voice, pushing through the surface formality.

"I'm just glad nobody's after you," he said. Her eyes held his, unwavering.

"Thank you, again," she said, turned quickly and hurried from the little dining room. He watched her go upstairs and then strolled outside, paused beside the desk clerk who was cleaning off the steps.

"Find out anything about that gunslinger last night?" he asked.

"Nope. Nobody knew him and nobody asked about him," the clerk said. "But then that's not uncommon here in Elbow Creek."

"I guess not," Fargo said and stepped out onto the street. His eyes moved slowly around the area, saw nothing to disturb him. He strolled to the stable and was happily surprised to see how much better the pinto's ankle appeared, the swelling almost gone with the suddenness that sometimes happens with pulled tendons. He lead-walked the horse again, then rubbed the pinto down and applied another rubbing of liniment.

"He might be ready for riding by tomorrow," the stable boy said.

Fargo nodded agreement. "What time does the post rider hit town usually?" he asked.

"Just about now," the boy said. "He's generally pretty much on time."

Fargo nodded and walked from the stable. He circled around to one side of the general store where the mail office took up one corner. He smiled quietly. She was there already, waiting as the mail clerk sorted through the contents of the pouch that had just been put on the counter. Fargo saw the clerk shake his head and Charity Keller turn, hurry back to the hotel, her face tight and troubled.

Once again, he should have turned away then, taken his curiosity in tow. But he hadn't. She'd become a riddle, a puzzle that intrigued. Besides, he hadn't another damn thing to do but wait around. This helped fill up time. And she was too damn pretty under all that formal properness to just forget about. But more important, she was in trouble. She knew that but she was trying to pull through alone or she'd no other way to turn. And she faced more than she could handle, he was certain. When the sharp-faced man didn't return to report his mission accomplished, his friends would come asking and find out. They wouldn't waste time waiting around, either.

Fargo strolled back to the hotel, sat down in the single, worn green chair in the lobby, pushed his hat down over his face, leaving only a slit of space to see under, and spent most of the afternoon there. When evening came and she still hadn't come down for dinner, he rose and stopped at the desk. "Where's Miss Keller?" he asked idly.

"She asked to have dinner sent up," the man said. "Waiter took it up a few minutes ago."

Fargo nodded thoughtfully and slowly mounted the steps. Charity Keller was scared and acting like a frightened rabbit, holing up to stay out of sight. Only it wouldn't do any good, he grimaced. He went to his room, lay down, his mind turning over probabilities. Weasel-face had been going to kill her, fast and cold-bloodedly. If his friends were going to take up where he left off they'd come in fast, put a hail of bullets into her, and hightail it. Charity Keller would be one more corpse passing through Elbow Creek, a hell of a lot more beautiful than most, but just as dead. Fargo stretched his arms over his head. He had another hour or two. They'd wait for the town to settle into its late-night routine when the only real activity would be down at The Happy Place. He let an hour go by, then a little more time, finally rose, checked the Colt, whirled it in his hand and returned it to the holster.

He went to the window of his room. He looked down onto the street and his jaw tightened at once. Six riders were reining to a halt in front of the hotel, one with a tan hat. He ran from the room and knocked hard at the girl's door. "It's Fargo," he said harshly. She opened in a moment, still dressed in the violet gown, he was glad to see. "Get your things. You're about to have company."

She stared at him for a moment, then spun, grabbed the

traveling bag. "This way, down the back stairs," he said, pulling her along. It was dark and he half-stumbled, caught himself, went on. He pushed the back door open and started outside with her, aware that she wasn't trying to ask any questions at all. But he'd underestimated the men. Two of them were just rounding the corner as he fled with the girl. He saw their hands go to their holsters and he flung the girl to the ground, let her fall freely as he hit the ground and rolled, came up firing a fusillade of shots. He saw the two men dive to the side, hit the ground, take cover behind the corner of the building. He leaped up, yanked the girl with him and ran. The other two, he knew, would soon be on their way.

"Where can we hide?" she gasped. He didn't have an answer as he ran, pulling her along. He heard shouts and curses from the darkness behind him. They were starting after him, guns out this time. He saw a feed barn, paused at the door. It was bolted tight.

"Damn," he muttered and ran on. The building loomed up on the right, soft lights reaching out from it—the Happy Place, with the tinkling of a piano faint in the air. He swerved, made a right angle, and headed at a full run for one of the side doors. He didn't see the puddle of water at the edge of the house and felt his feet go out from under him as he hit it. He twisted his body as he fell, landing on his right arm. The Colt skittered out of his hand and, in horror, he saw it slide into a drainpipe that led under the side of the house.

"Goddamn," he swore as he stared at the drain. There wasn't time to search for it now. He pulled himself up and yanked open the side door.

"In here?" he heard the girl say.

"In here, dammit," he repeated, pulled her after him, up the darkened steps to the second floor. He paused at a door, the sounds from behind it unmistakable, went on to the next. He'd listened at four doors before he found an empty room, pushed the girl into it, and then swore silently. And he was still in the room now, lying half-atop her, naked as a jaybird, wondering if they'd both feel the thud of a hail of bullets. Dammit, if it didn't work he'd at least die doing what he most enjoyed, Fargo swore at himself as he moved atop her, pressing up to the warm, furrowed portal.

"No," she gasped, tried to wriggle back. "You're just taking advantage," she breathed.

He heard the footsteps at the door. "Use your damn mouth for something better," he hissed, pressed his lips on hers and pushed his torso forward. The furrow parted, surprising wetness, warm welcoming. She gasped, a sharp cry, tried to twist away. Her legs opened and closed around him, tightening, falling open again. He pushed deeper, slowly, back and forth. "Ooooh, oh, oh," she gasped through the pressure of his mouth. He heard the door open behind him, felt the men in the doorway. He pressed harder in her and her hips lifted, the senses refusing all resistance, welcoming, hungering. Her protests under his lips sounded like gasps of unquestioned pleasure. Her eyes were wide, staring up at him, a whirlpool of emotions she could no longer control.

He moved again, increased speed, and heard her long cry, covered one full breast with his hand. His ears caught another sound, the door closing, the footsteps hurrying away outside in the hallway. He paused for a moment, then thrust upwards again, letting his lips find her breasts.

"Oh, God," she gasped. "Oh, oh." Then he felt her hands tighten into fists. "No, damn you," she hissed, struck at him, opened her hands to claw at him. He avoided her nails, rolled away from her, and she scooted crab-fashion up the bed to the wall. He watched her as she gasped in deep breaths, her lovely breasts moving up and down, the tiny pink tips still firm. "Bastard," she flung at him. "You didn't have to do that."

"I had to make sure they'd buy it," he said.

"Bastard," she repeated. "You took advantage. You could have faked it."

"Couldn't take the chance," he said blandly. "Besides, I'm no good at faking some things."

She glared at him, still drawing in deep breaths. Her eyes went down to his huge, still vibrant organ, tore away almost unhappily. She reached down, her round little rear sticking up, felt under the bed with one hand. He leaned forward, brought his palm down hard on the delicious little mound. The slap resounded in the little room and she yelped as she whirled back, the violet dress in one hand. She pulled it up in front of her, deep-blue eyes flashing fire at him.

"What was that for, damn you?" she snapped.

"For lying to me yesterday," he said. "And for damn near

getting me shot full of lead while naked." He reached one hand out, pulled her up to a sitting position as she kept the dress in front of her. "Now, you're going to tell me what the hell you're all about, honey," he growled.

Ⓢ

Wild Westerns From SIGNET

*Price slightly higher in Canada

Buy them at your local

bookstore or use coupon

on next page for ordering.

SIGNET Double Westerns For Your Library

SIGNET BRAND WESTERNS BY FRANK O'ROURKE

		(0451)
☐	**WARBONNET LAW**	(111311—$1.95)
☐	**GUNSMOKE OVER BIG MUDDY**	(111338—$1.95)
☐	**VIOLENCE AT SUNDOWN**	(111346—$1.95)
☐	**GUN HAND**	(111354—$1.75)
☐	**LATIGO**	(111362—$1.75)
☐	**BANDOLIER CROSSING**	(111370—$1.75)
☐	**LEGEND IN THE DUST**	(111389—$1.75)
☐	**BLACKWATER**	(111397—$1.95)
☐	**DAKOTA RIFLE**	(111400—$1.95)
☐	**THE BIG FIFTY**	(111419—$1.75)
☐	**GOLD UNDER SKULL PEAK**	(111427—$1.75)
☐	**ACTION AT THREE PEAKS**	(111443—$1.95)
☐	**VIOLENT COUNTRY**	(111451—$1.75)
☐	**HIGH VENGEANCE**	(111435—$1.75)
☐	**AMBUSCADE**	(094905—$1.75)*
☐	**DESPERATE RIDER**	(095340—$1.75)

*Price slightly higher in Canada

Buy them at your local

bookstore or use coupon

on next page for ordering.

86-51

SIGNET Americana Novels of Interest